KT-219-878

Accla**im** for the book

**ARIEL S. WINTER!**

"It's the author's ambition that attracts…his sense of reaching beyond our expectations of what a book like ·this (or really, any book) can do…[A] triumph."
—*Los Angeles Times*

"Not content with writing one first novel like ordinary mortals, Ariel Winter has written three—and in the style of some of the most famous crime writers of all time, for good measure. It's a virtuoso act of literary recreation that's both astonishingly faithful and wildly, audaciously original. One hell of a debut."
—*James Frey*

"Massive and marvelous…it's difficult not to feel a little spellbound by *The Twenty-Year Death*."
—*Washington Post*

"*The Twenty-Year Death* is a bravura debut, ingenious and assured, and a fitting tribute to the trio of illustrious ghosts who are looking—with indulgence, surely—over Ariel Winter's shoulder."
—*John Banville*

"This is audacious and astonishingly executed. What may seem at first like an amusing exercise for crime fiction buffs becomes by the end immersive, exhilarating, and revelatory."
—*Booklist*

Pelleter plunged forward, almost twisting his ankle on one of the cobblestones, running after nothing, since there was nothing visible ahead of him.

He passed other openings, any one of which his man could have taken, and so he slowed his pace, trying to hear the other man's footsteps over his own labored breathing. Running through back alleys was a young man's work. Pelleter was no longer young.

He stopped, but heard nothing but his own body's protest.

An oval ceramic tile screwed into the side of one of the buildings read "Rue Victor Hugo." The provincialism of this almost made him laugh. To have a Rue Victor Hugo had apparently been deemed necessary, but that Verargent had settled on this back alley for the designation was small-town politics in its most essential form.

He waited another moment, straining for some sign, and then he turned back.

As he did a large form materialized out of one of the doorways and brought both hands down on the back of the chief inspector's neck, dropping Pelleter to his knees. A sharp jolt of pain shot from his kneecaps into his stomach, which threatened to empty itself.

The man swung again, still a two-fisted blow, this one landing across the chief inspector's cheek...

# The Twenty-Year Death:
# MALNIVEAU PRISON

### by Ariel S. Winter

A HARD CASE CRIME NOVEL

**A HARD CASE CRIME BOOK**
(HCC-108-X)
*First Hard Case Crime edition: July 2014*

Published by

Titan Books
A division of Titan Publishing Group Ltd
144 Southwark Street
London SE1 0UP

in collaboration with Winterfall LLC

Print edition ISBN 978-1-78116-793-9
E-book ISBN 978-1-78116-886-8

Design direction by Max Phillips
*www.maxphillips.net*

Typeset by Swordsmith Productions

The name "Hard Case Crime" and the Hard Case Crime logo
are trademarks of Winterfall LLC. Hard Case Crime books are
selected and edited by Charles Ardai.

Printed in the United States of America

*Visit us on the web at www.HardCaseCrime.com*

*in memoriam G.S. with apologies*

# MALNIVEAU PRISON

# I.

## A Man in the Street

The rain started with no warning. It had been dark for an hour by then, and the night had masked the accumulation of clouds. But once it began, the raindrops fell with such violence that everyone in Verargent felt oppressed.

After forty minutes of constant drumming—it was near eight o'clock, Tuesday, April 4, 1931—the rain eased some, settling into the steady spring rainfall that would continue throughout the night.

The rain's new tenor allowed for other sounds. The baker, on his way to bed for the night, heard the lapping of a large body of water from behind his basement door. He shot back the lock, and rushed downstairs to find nearly two feet of water covering the basement floor. A gushing stream ran down the wall that faced the street.

Appalled, the baker rushed up the stairs calling to his wife. She hurried past him, down the stairs, to see for herself, as he went to the coat rack to retrieve his black rain slicker. This had happened before. Something blocked the gutter at the side of the street, and the water was redirected down their drive, flooding the basement. Somebody in Town Hall would hear from him in the morning.

He opened the front door and went out into the rain just as his wife arrived from the basement. The force of the storm pressed the hood of his slicker over his forehead. He hurried down the drive with his head bowed;

rivulets of water formed long v's on the packed earth beneath his feet. Now he'd be up much of the night bailing
out the basement, and he had to be up at three-thirty to
make the bread. The mayor would hear about this in the
morning!

He reached the end of the drive, about twenty-five
feet, and looked along the curb towards the opening to the
sewer. The streetlamps were not lit, but there appeared to
be a person lying in the gutter. The baker cursed all drunks.

"Hey!" he called, approaching the man, who was lying
face down. The baker's voice was almost covered by the
rain. "Hey, you!" He kicked the man's foot. There was no
response. The street was dark. No one else was out in the
storm. The houses across the way and along the street
were shuttered. He kicked the man again, cursing him.
Water still coursed along the drive towards his house.

His schedule was shot; tomorrow was going to be a
nightmare. Then he noticed that the drunk's face was
buried in the water coursing around his body, and the
baker felt the first flicker of panic.

He knelt, soaking his pants leg. The rain felt like pins
and needles against his shoulders. Choking back his discomfort, he reached for the drunk's shoulder, and rolled
him away from the curb so that he was lying on his back
in the street. The drunk's head rolled to the side. His eyes
were open; his face was bloated. He was undisturbed by
the rain.

The baker jerked back. The concrete thought: *He's dead!*
coincided with a gathering numbness and the uncomfortable beat of his heart in his throat. The baker turned, and
hurried back to the house.

His wife, elbows cupped in opposite hands, held herself at the door. "Did you fix it?"

"Call the police," the baker said.

His wife went to the phone stand at the foot of the stairs. "You're dripping on the floor; take off your coat."

"Call the police," the baker said, not explaining himself. "Call the police, call the police."

His wife raised the phone to her ear. "The line's down. It must be the storm."

The baker turned and grabbed the doorknob.

"Where are you going? The basement…"

"There's a man dead in the street."

The baker lived ten minutes from Town Hall, which was also the police station. Nervous, he avoided looking at the dead man as he turned towards the center of town. The rain was still steady, a static hush over everything that served to both cloud and concentrate the baker's hurried thoughts: A man was dead. The basement was flooded. It was late. A man was dead.

At the police station, he found that it would not have mattered if the phone lines had been operational. Of the three officers on duty, two had been called to assist with an automobile crash before the phone lines had gone down.

"The rain makes the roads treacherous," the remaining officer explained. "People shouldn't be out."

"But the man's dead," the baker insisted, confused that these words had not inspired a flurry of activity.

"We just have to wait for Martin and Arnaud to return."

The baker sat on one of the three wooden chairs that

lined the wall between the front door and the counter where the officer sat. Small puddles of water refracted on the tile, tracing the steps the baker had taken since entering the police station. The officer had already taken his name and statement, and now was trying to pass the time, but the baker was unable to focus. He was exhausted.

Martin and Arnaud returned twenty minutes later. They were young men, the fronts of their slickers covered in mud from their recent work at the automobile crash. They glanced at the baker, but ignored him, talking to each other, until the officer on duty interrupted them and explained the baker's situation.

It was decided that Martin would accompany the baker back to his house, while Arnaud would go in the police car to the hospital to retrieve a medic and an ambulance.

Back out in the rain, the men were silent. The streets were still deserted. Even the few late-night cafés and bars at the center of town were closed. Martin and the baker arrived at the baker's house to find the body unmoved. It was still blocking the gutter, still sending water into the baker's home. They stood several feet away in silence, their hands in the pockets of their slickers, their shoulders hunched against the rain.

They only had to wait a minute before a police car followed by an ambulance pulled up in front of the house. The medics jumped out of the ambulance and retrieved a stretcher from the back. Arnaud came to where Martin and the baker were standing.

"We will contact you tomorrow, if we need anything else," Martin said.

The baker watched the medics load the body onto the stretcher and then into the ambulance.

"Somebody needs to fix the drainage," the baker said, his mind clearing some now that the body had been removed.

"You'll have to bring that up with the town in the morning."

"I have to be up early, and my basement is flooded."

The officers were unconcerned.

The baker's heart wasn't really in it.

The ambulance pulled away. One of the officers said, "We'll let you know," but he didn't say what they would let him know. They got back into the police car and pulled away, leaving the street once again empty.

The baker could see that the water was already flowing correctly, draining into the sewer. He turned back up his drive, preparing for a night bailing out the basement.

Inside, his wife came downstairs. "What happened?"

The baker peeled off his dripping coat, and began to roll up the sleeves of his shirt. "Some drunk was taken unexpected."

These were the details as related over breakfast the next morning to Chief Inspector Pelleter by the Verargent chief of police Letreau. Pelleter was in town to hear the testimony of a murderer at the nearby Malniveau Prison. This murderer, Mahossier, was one that Pelleter had arrested several years earlier for a brutal multiple child slaying in which he had kept children in cages in his basement in order to have them fight one another to the

death. On two prior occasions, Mahossier had contacted
Pelleter, claiming to have information. Pelleter hated to
be on call to a convicted criminal, but Mahossier would
talk to no one else, and his information had both times
proved accurate. Over the course of the previous visits,
Pelleter and chief of police Letreau had become friendly.

As they ate, the rain streamed down the café windows,
distorting the town square, rendering it invisible.

The café was empty of other customers. The proprietor stood behind the counter with his arms crossed,
watching the water run. Two electric wall sconces had
been lit in deference to the continued storm.

An automobile passed around the square, its dark form
like some kind of lumbering animal, its engine sawing
diligently, audible and then gone.

Nobody was out who didn't have to be, and not many
people had to be out in Verargent early on a Wednesday
morning. The weather had been worse last night. Why
would a drunk choose to be out in the rain instead of sitting it out in some bar?

"Tell me about the dead man," Pelleter said.

"We don't know him. None of my men had seen him
before, and in a small town like this, you get to know the
faces of all the night owls. He had no documents on him,
no billfold, no money. Just a drifter. We've sent his fingerprints in to see if there are any matches."

"You get many drifters here?"

"No."

Pelleter sat back and retrieved a cigar from his inner
coat pocket. He lit it, and blew out a steady stream of
smoke.

"Would you go with me to see the baker?" Letreau asked.

Pelleter chewed his cigar. Seeing Pelleter smoking, the proprietor came to clear the plates. The two lawmen waited for him to leave.

"I need to get to Malniveau. Madame Pelleter expects me home."

"It won't be a minute. This is exactly what it looks like, a drifter drowning in a puddle. I just need to be careful, and if I arrive with you, an inspector from the city, if there's anything to know, we'll know it. Benoît will be too scared to hide anything."

The rain continued outside.

"Not that I think he has anything to hide. I just need to be careful."

"Tell me about the baker."

"Benoît? He made the bread we just ate. His father was the baker here before him, but the old man died many years ago. He works seven days a week, and does little outside of his house and his shop. In his domain, he can seem very commanding, but when you see him anywhere else, at the market, at the cinema, he is a small man. My men said he sat last night in the station as though he had been called to the headmaster's office at school. And he's fifteen years older than my oldest officer! His wife works in the bakery too."

Pelleter called the proprietor over to pay, but Letreau told him that it was taken care of.

"I have a tab," he explained, standing.

Pelleter made sure that his cigar had gone out, and then placed it back in his pocket. He took his rain slicker from the standing coat rack just inside the door, and his hat.

Letreau called goodbye to the proprietor, who answered as though he had just been awakened. Fixing his own coat, Letreau said, "I hate to go out in this rain." Then he opened the door, and the sound of the weather doubled in strength, like turning up the radio.

There were more people on the street than it had appeared from the café, but each walked separately with the determination of someone who had places to go. Most walked with hunched shoulders and heads down, but there was the occasional umbrella.

The bronze statue atop the ten-foot concrete column in the center of the square watched the faces of the shops on the north side of the street.

It was cold.

The two men walked in silence. Letreau led, but they walked so close together it would have been impossible to say whether or not Pelleter knew where they were going. They crossed the square, and took the southern of the two roads that entered the square from the west. The buildings here were still a mixture of shops and houses. The baker's shop was on the first floor of a two-story brick building, five storefronts from the square. The words *Benoît and Son Bakery* were emblazoned on the plate glass window in green and gold paint.

There were several women in the store buying bread for the day, but when Benoît saw the policemen enter, he came out from behind the counter. "Monsieur Letreau! I'm glad you came. This terrible business from last night has my wife very upset. She could hardly sleep. And we have to get up very early. Very early to make the bread. We could hardly sleep."

Despite his loud greeting, the baker looked exhausted, the spaces under his eyes dark and puffy. There was a small patch of light stubble on the left side of his chin at the jaw line where he had missed a spot shaving.

"And my basement is ruined. One day my house will collapse. You'll see. The town must do something about this. Every time that gutter gets clogged, I must spend the next two days bailing out my own house. The worms come through the walls."

The customers conducted their business with Madame Benoît, the women apparently used to the baker's little tirades. As each one left, the sound of the bell hanging from the top of the door mixed with the shush of the rain.

"This is Chief Inspector Pelleter," Letreau said. "He's come to see about this business."

Pelleter was annoyed by the introduction. He could see himself becoming more involved in this investigation than he wanted to be. He moved his lips, but it was unclear what the expression meant.

Benoît stepped in towards the two men. "Is it that serious?" Then he got excited. "Or are you here to inspect our sewers, and solve this problem? I can take you to my house right away. My wife can take care of things here. There's still water in my basement. Let me show you."

"I'm with the Central Police," Pelleter said.

Benoît became grave again. "What happened?"

"Nothing as far as we know," Letreau said. "We just wanted to hear it again from you."

The door opened. The bell tinkled, letting the last customer out. Madame Benoît watched the three men, but she remained behind the counter.

"I was going to bed when I thought to check the basement. As I said, these storms often cause floods. When I saw the water, I rushed out to the street, and found the drunk lying there. We tried to call the police, but the lines were down, so I went to the station myself. It probably caused another two feet of water, leaving that body there like that."

"The men said he was face-up when they got there."

"He had been face-down. I rolled him over to see if he was all right. Then I saw he was dead…"

"Did you hear anything? See anything?"

Benoît gripped his left hand in his right, rubbing the knuckles. His voice had grown much quieter, almost timid, and he glanced at his wife before looking back at Pelleter. "What was there to hear? Only the rain… Only the rain…"

Benoît turned to his wife. "Did you hear anything last night?" he called to her.

She pressed her lips together, and shook her head.

Letreau caught Pelleter's eye, and Pelleter nodded once.

"Okay, Benoît," Letreau said. "That's fine."

"Did…" Benoît looked at his wife again. "Was… Did something…happen? The man was drunk, right?"

"Sure. As far as we know."

Benoît's expression eased slightly at that. He had clearly

been shaken very badly by the whole incident, and the idea that something more might have taken place was too much for him.

"Ah, the mop!" he said looking down. "We need the mop."

The door opened, letting in another customer, and before it closed a second new customer snuck in as well. They commented on the terrible weather.

Benoît looked for permission to go, and Letreau said, "Thank you. We'll let you know if we need anything."

Benoît stepped back, his expression even more natural now. He reached one hand out behind him for the mop, which was still several feet away in a corner behind the counter. "Come to my house, and I'll show you the flood. The water was up to here." He indicated just below his knees with his hand.

Pelleter opened the door, and Letreau followed him out into the street.

"What do you think?"

"There's nothing to think."

"I just had to be sure."

Pelleter nodded his approval. Water sloshed off of the brim of his hat.

They began to walk back towards the square. "Come back to the station. I'll drive you to the prison."

They waited for an automobile to pass, and then they crossed the street. The rain had eased some again, but it was still steady. Lights could be seen in the windows of various buildings. It was like a perpetual dusk even though it was still before ten in the morning.

They stepped into the police station through the entrance on the side street beside Town Hall. The station was an open space separated into two sections by a counter. In front of the counter was a small entryway with several chairs. Behind the counter were three desks arranged to just fit the space. Doors led to offices along the back and left-hand wall. Letreau needed to get keys to one of the police cars.

"Chief," the young man behind the counter said. "There's a message for you." The officer looked at Pelleter, and then back at his commanding officer. Pelleter had never seen the man before, but it was obvious that the young officer knew who he was.

"This is Officer Martin," Letreau said to Pelleter. "He's the one who went out to the baker's house last night." Then to Martin as he started behind the counter towards his office, "Did we get an ID on our dead drifter?"

"Not yet," the man said. "It was the hospital."

Letreau stopped and looked back.

The young man picked up a piece of paper from the desk on which he had written the message, but he didn't need to look at it. It was more to steady himself. "Cause of death was multiple stab wounds to stomach and chest. No water in the lungs."

Pelleter looked across at Letreau who was looking at him. Letreau's face had gone pale. His drunken drifter had just turned into a homicide. And no water in the lungs meant the man had been dead before he ended up in the gutter.

The young officer looked up. He swallowed when he saw the chief's face.

"Anything else?" Letreau barked.

"There were no holes in his clothes," the officer said. "Someone stabbed him to death, and then changed his outfit."

# 2.

## *Malniveau Prison*

The sudden silence in the station was stunning. It was made all the more awkward when two other officers appeared from the back, laughing over some shared joke.

They saw the state of the room and fell silent as well.

Letreau stepped heavily across the small space to the counter, and took the message from out of the desk officer's hand. "I have to call the hospital," he said, and disappeared into his office, slamming the door behind him.

Pelleter saw Martin look up at him, but he turned away, uninterested in any paternal conversation. He retrieved the cigar he had started at the café from his pocket, lit it, and took the seat that the baker had occupied the night before.

The two officers who had been joking returned to their respective desks.

Pelleter concentrated on the fine taste of the smoke from his cigar. He opened his coat. Light drops of water continued to fall on the floor around him.

If Letreau was going to be long, he would have to take a taxi. Visiting hours at the prison were short. The warden refused to be accommodating, annoyed by Pelleter's visits. He felt that they were unprofessional, that the prisoners, once under his guard, were dead to the outside world. Pelleter's own displeasure for these visits didn't soften the warden's opinion.

The three officers talked amongst themselves in quiet tones. A murder in this town was big news.

Pelleter looked at his cigar as he blew out a plume of smoke. It was more than half gone.

Letreau's office door opened. The officers fell silent, but he ignored them as he strode across the station to the door. "Come," he said to Pelleter. "Let's go."

Pelleter stood. It was obvious that Letreau was distraught, his easy nature covered by a set jaw and a gruff manner. "I can take a taxi."

"No. There's nothing to be done right now. Let's go."

They went back out into the rain to one of the police cars parked just outside the station. The doors had been left unlocked. Letreau got behind the wheel and Pelleter sat beside him in the passenger seat.

Letreau started the car, turning on the windshield wiper, and then he pulled out of the spot, and headed east out of town.

"Any news?" Pelleter said.

"Just what you heard."

The two men remained silent for the remainder of the half-hour drive.

When the town fell away, it was replaced by fields that extended beyond the wire fences on either side of the road. There was the occasional outlying farmhouse or barn. Cows milled in a large enclosure, the hair on their undersides hanging in muddy clumps matted by the rain. Even in the countryside all colors were muted and everything seemed pinned down by the spring gale. The sky was large and gray.

The prison was visible ten minutes before they arrived there. It was a heavy, awkward structure imposed on the land, a dark blotch. It appeared a remnant from some earlier age.

They pulled into the drive. A guard, so bundled as to be indiscernible, appeared from the guard house, waved at them, and went to open the twenty-foot iron gate.

"A man could kill himself here," Letreau said, "and no one would blame him."

The guard had the gate open. Letreau pulled the police car through, and the guard waved again, but Pelleter still could not make the man out.

There were several other vehicles—a truck, two police cars, three civilian cars—parked in the small cobblestone courtyard before the front entrance. There was another courtyard in the center of the building where the prisoners took their exercise. The narrow windows in the stone walls were impenetrable black slits, dead eyes watching over them.

"There's something wrong about having this place out here," Letreau said, parking the car. "The men they put here come from far away, from other places. That way the rest of the country can forget about them. And my town is the closest. All the men who work in the prison live in Verargent. Don't you think they bring some of this back to town with them? We're a peace-loving community. Most of our complaints are petty thefts and the occasional late-night drunk."

Pelleter didn't point out that somebody had been murdered in town the night before. After all, Letreau was right.

"It looks this bad on a sunny day too. I hate coming out here."

At the front door, there was a loud clank as the lock was released, and then the door was opened to admit them. It was musty inside, and the only light came from two exposed light bulbs high on the wall.

"I'll take your coats, gentlemen," the guard said.

"How are you today, Remy?" Letreau asked the guard.

"I'm still alive, Chief," the guard said, hanging the coats in a small booth just inside the door.

"There's always that."

Pelleter pushed open the door to the administrative offices, while Letreau stayed to talk a moment with the guard. Nothing had changed in the two years since Pelleter had been there last. It was the same large room with two rows of desks down the center. The same filing cabinets lined the walls. The same people sat behind the desks. The same drab paint reflected the electric bulbs hanging from the ceiling.

The warden, a large gray-haired man, must have been informed that Pelleter was there, since he was waiting with a look of impatience just inside the door. He managed to use his irritation to add to his air of importance.

"Inspector Pelleter. I'm so glad. If you had been even five minutes more, we would have missed each other. I have promised my wife a holiday in the city, and she is expecting me an hour ago."

A neat, sharp-angled man stood with his hands crossed in front of him just behind the warden.

"Let me introduce Monsieur Fournier. I don't believe you've met. Fournier is the Assistant Warden here now. He takes care of the jobs I don't want to."

Fournier took Pelleter's hand. "He jests."

None of the men smiled.

"Fournier will be in charge while I am away, and he will be more than capable of assisting you with anything you need. Not that you need much assistance. You are an old hand at this." The warden smiled at that, but it was an expression of pure malice. "You could have probably gone to get the prisoner yourself."

He looked around the office. The people at the desks made an effort to focus on their paperwork, but they were clearly uncomfortable.

"I really must be going." He looked at his watch and then the clock on the wall. "I shouldn't have even stopped to say hello. Fournier, you have everything you need."

"Yes, *Monsieur le Directeur*."

The warden stepped towards his office, but stopped when the outer door opened to reveal Letreau.

"Chief Letreau," the warden said, and he glanced at Fournier, confused and accusatory. "Nothing is wrong, I trust."

Letreau paused in the doorway, surprised at being addressed so suddenly. He looked at Pelleter, but Pelleter was unreadable. "As Remy says, I'm still alive."

"Yes," the warden said, almost sneering as he took possession of himself. "There's always that."

Letreau stepped in and greeted the other people in the office including Fournier.

The warden excused himself, and disappeared into his office.

"If you'll follow me, Chief Inspector," Fournier said. They left the administrative offices, and went down a barren hallway. Fournier conducted himself with an icy precision throughout. "I understand you have been here before."

"This will be my third visit."

"The warden feels you give this man too much credit and that you make him feel important. It is our job to be sure that these men do not feel important. They are criminals."

Pelleter said nothing. He retrieved his partially smoked cigar from his pocket and put it between his lips without lighting it.

"There is no question that there is a certain intelligence in some of them, and that their crimes require guts. Perhaps in another time they would have been something else. But here they are still criminals. They are to be punished, not applauded. And it is dangerous to make any of them feel important."

They were outside one of the visiting rooms, which also served as interrogation rooms if needed. "Is that what the warden says?"

"It's what I say," Fournier said, his expression unchanged. He unlocked the door with a key on a large ring. "Wait here."

Pelleter paused, but resisted asking Fournier if he knew

just what Mahossier had done. The assistant warden hadn't seen the way those children had been brutalized. A man who could do that felt important all on his own.

Pelleter went into the room. The door closed behind him, and his jaw clenched around his cigar at the clang. The room was devoid of any distinguishing features, just stone below, above, and all around. No sounds penetrated the walls. If this was not enough punishment for a criminal, than Pelleter didn't know what was.

The door opened only a moment later, and two guards led Mahossier in. He was a small old man, bald, with deep wrinkles across his forehead, and a beaked nose. His hands had been cuffed in front of him, and another set of cuffs chained his legs together. These had been linked by a third chain between the two. The guards sat Mahossier in the seat across from Pelleter.

Fournier had also come in with the three other men. "We will be right outside the door. If he tries—"

"We'll be fine," Pelleter interrupted.

"But if—"

"We'll be fine."

Fournier flared his nostrils, the first time he had allowed his emotions to be seen.

"The Chief Inspector and I go way back," Mahossier said, his eyes locked on Fournier, his voice so quiet it was almost soothing.

Fournier nodded to the guards, and the three men left the room, closing the door behind them and engaging the lock.

"How's Madame Pelleter?" Mahossier said.

Pelleter moved his cigar from one side of his mouth to

the other. Facing the man, it was all he could do to keep the images of those children out of his mind.

Mahossier seemed to know it.

"Still no children?" Mahossier smiled. "But, of course... That ship has sailed. It's much too late for you now. Such a shame. Children really make the world worth living in." His eyebrows furrowed and his lips fell in a theatrical frown. "Of course, there are never any children here." His expression went cold. "Plenty of rain though."

Pelleter bit his cigar again. He'd have to light it soon just to help him breathe.

"But of course, even if it's too late for Madame Pelleter, it's not too late for you. A Chief Inspector! Plenty of young girls out there. Someone to take care of you in your old age. Think of it!"

Mahossier's excitement at his own fantasy took him over, and he looked up, almost overjoyed. The chains weighing him down were nothing to him. He looked back at Pelleter.

"So how is Madame Pelleter? Well, I trust."

Pelleter waited patiently. It wouldn't do to rush him. If Mahossier thought that he was getting a reaction from the inspector, then he would go on forever.

"How do you like this room? You must...they keep putting you in it. It's much like mine, although I do have a little window." He held up his right hand, which forced him to draw his left hand with it because of the cuffs, and he indicated a narrow space with his thumb and fore-finger. "It's a small window, but at least it's a window. And I have you to thank...Thank you...Thank you...I must have you up some time. You should tell the warden that

you are more than welcome…Or Fournier. But then he'll
think I like you, he's not as smart as you, he wouldn't know
you're not my type."

He looked up again, and it made the wrinkles in his
forehead even deeper.

Pelleter chose to light his cigar. He took his time about
it, ignoring the chained man across from him, extracting
a single match from his pocket, scratching it on the table,
and taking several puffs, making sure the cigar was really
lit. Mahossier watched in silence.

"Okay, I understand you." His expression had turned
serious. "And it's not as though Fournier will leave me in
here forever. The rules are the rules are the rules are the
rules…But it's safer in here with you than it is out there…
You've had more than one chance to kill me, but I'm still
here." He tapped his chest, and the chains jingled together.

"There's a first for everything," Pelleter said. The smoke
from his cigar hung in the air between them.

"Well said! Right to my point. That's why I can talk to
you. Your wife is a very lucky woman…Still no children?"
He raised his eyebrows, but then shrugged when the
inspector made no response. "Here is the thing—there
are fewer of us than there were before…At first it was
just one, but now it's two, three, four…I don't really know,
it's a big prison and they don't let me out all that often."
His theatrical frown again. "Glamieux's gone. He was
another one of yours, right? They slit his throat. And
there have been others."

"What's that have to do with me? People get killed in
prison all the time."

"Not all the time…not all the time…Sometimes. Not that often, actually. Not many people in one month. Not many people and nothing's done about it, said about it… outside. Even here."

"What's the warden say?"

"What does the warden say?"

The two men watched each other, both calm, but each in his own way. Pelleter smoked. Mahossier smiled.

"We need somebody on the outside. Someone we can trust… Someone like you. There should at least be an inquiry."

"You want an inquiry into several dead prisoners?"

"They *were* people too." Mahossier's theatricality undermined any sense of real feeling in his expression. It was chilling as always.

Pelleter leaned forward. "You want an inquiry?" He stood up. "That's easy. Let's have an inquiry. Fournier's right here. He's Assistant Warden. He'll know." Pelleter was at the door now, his hand raised to knock on the door. "I'll ask him about all these dead prisoners. He doesn't seem to like the lot of you very much, but if someone's killing you…" He motioned to knock. "Let's inquire."

"Please don't do that," Mahossier said. His voice was still quiet and even, and for that reason it was commanding.

Pelleter let his hand drop. "Is there nothing to inquire about then?"

"It's just that there are the right people to inquire it of."

The two men stared at one another. Mahossier's face remained self-assured, Pelleter's steely. The last time Pelleter had come out here, Mahossier had given him the information necessary to capture a murderess in a case that was nearly three years cold.

He waited for Mahossier to say something else, but the prisoner just sat looking up at him, the lines in his forehead drawing deeper as he widened his eyes in mock innocence. It certainly felt as though he was simply making trouble, but it wouldn't hurt to ask a few questions. Pelleter could always turn it over to the central prison commission, if need be.

Pelleter waited a moment longer and then turned and knocked on the door. There was the sound of the key in the lock.

"Send my regards to Madame Pelleter," Mahossier said behind him.

The door opened, and Pelleter stepped out of the tiny room.

Fournier didn't ask what Mahossier had said as he led Pelleter back to the front offices. It was hard to know if this was out of professionalism, a show of contempt, or a genuine lack of interest. The man was so particular in every movement that it was hard to read him at all.

Letreau stood as they came into the front office. "Ready?"

"Yes."

"Please let me know if you need anything else," Fournier said.

"I'm sure I will. Send my regards again to your boss."

"Yes, I'm sure he regrets that he could not stay. His wife can be really insistent sometimes."

They shook hands, and went out to retrieve their coats from Remy.

"So?" Letreau said as he slipped his on.

"We'll see," Pelleter said, and then to Remy, "Have you had many prisoners die recently?"

Remy thought about it, helping the inspector with his coat. "There was one about two months ago."

"Disease?"

"Stabbing, I think." Then he shrugged. "People die anywhere, I guess."

"Any others?"

Remy shook his head. "I don't know. There have been other stabbings, if that's what you mean. But that happens."

Pelleter pressed his lips together. There was no way to know what he was thinking.

Outside, the rain was still coming down strong. The two men hastened to their car, and slammed the doors behind them. It was hot and humid in the car, adding to the general sense of discomfort.

"Have you heard anything about prisoners dying?"

"No," Letreau said, starting the car. "But I might not have. It's not really our business."

"Where would they get buried?"

"Depends on where they're from, I guess."

"But you haven't heard of any bodies getting shipped out on the train?"

Letreau shook his head. "No. But that doesn't mean anything."

"No, it doesn't." Pelleter looked out the window.

"Is that what Mahossier got you out here about?"

"Yes."

"You think it's anything?"

"I don't know."

They remained silent the rest of the trip, but this time Pelleter didn't see the wet landscape before him, didn't see the barns, or the cows, or even notice when the town started up again.

When they pulled in front of the station, the rain had eased up enough so that they could get out of the car without hunching their shoulders.

"Are you going back to the city tonight?" Letreau said.

"I don't know."

"If you stay around, my wife wouldn't hear of you having dinner anywhere else."

"Thank you."

Letreau waited, and then he went into the station. Pelleter followed him.

The same young officer, Martin, was behind the desk. He didn't even wait for the chief to get around the counter before saying, "Another message for you, Chief."

Letreau crossed and took the paper before the officer could say another thing. "This just gets worse."

Pelleter came up behind him, and looked at the paper.

The fingerprints of the dead man had turned up in the system. His name was Marcel Meranger. He had a long record as a safecracker who had worked with a number of the large crime cartels around the country.

This meant that there could be any number of people who would want to kill him.

The only problem was the last note taken down in the young officer's looping hand.

Marcel Meranger had been arrested thirteen years ago and sentenced to forty years in prison.

The prison was Malniveau.

# 3.

## *The American Writer*

Letreau rushed into his office, leaving Pelleter holding the paper with the message. Once there, he picked up the phone and could be heard barking, "Hello…Get me Fournier…"

Pelleter approached the young officer who had taken the message, still seated at the front counter. He pointed to the phone. "May I?"

The young officer, surprised that he had even been asked for permission, nodded, and managed a "But of course."

Pelleter spoke to the operator and hung up.

Letreau could be heard saying, "This is a problem, and it's your problem…"

"Has anyone ever escaped from Malniveau?"

The young officer was startled again at having been addressed. He had clearly been eavesdropping on the chief's conversation. "Not in my memory and I've lived here my whole life," the young officer said. "But when we were kids they used to talk about the three great escapes since the prison's been open."

"Three?"

The officer nodded. "In the 1820s sometime a man faked consumption. He coughed and coughed for days. Then he cut his fingers on the rocks and used the blood to stain the front of his shirt so that it looked like he'd been coughing up his lungs… Of course the warden didn't want to infect his whole population enclosed like that, so he ordered that the man be brought into town where he was to be quarantined in an old shed…He escaped as soon as he was in town. There was no train here then so he had to go on foot or get a ride and he didn't want to risk getting a ride, so he didn't get very far before they caught him…He was in solitary for good after that."

Pelleter looked across to Letreau in his office, who was pacing as he spoke, the phone cord making a mess of the papers on his desk.

"And the other two?"

"The second wasn't really an escape. One of the men who worked in the laundry hid himself among the sheets that were to be discarded. Rather typical, I guess. Of course, the sheets were checked before they were taken out the front gate and the man was found, so he didn't even make it beyond the prison walls."

Letreau was shouting now in the other room. "You listen, Fournier. You better find a way to get in touch with your boss, because he's looking at a scandal that may lose him his job!"

The young officer ignored the commotion behind him, flattered at the attention the chief inspector was giving him.

"The last escape was during the war. By then the prisoners were allowed some exercise time outside in the courtyard. Three men got together and planned their escape…They arranged themselves so they would be the

last out in the courtyard with a guard just behind them…
As the last man stepped out into the fresh air, all three
fell back and overpowered the guard, taking his gun and
forcing their way back into the prison using the guard as a
hostage. They made their way to the front gate, but the
warden had a chance to arrange a team of guards outside.
They killed two of the prisoners on sight, and the third
one surrendered claiming that they had just wanted a
chance to serve in the war. He was sent to the trenches
and killed there. If he'd just waited that would probably
have happened anyway."

"So none actually made it."

"Never."

"Do you think that one could have now?"

"Not without help."

"That's what I think too."

Pelleter touched his hand to his mouth.

"Chief Inspector?"

Pelleter focused on the young officer.

"You went to see Mahossier…I mean, you caught
Mahossier. You know the man. What kind of a man could
do—?"

Officer Martin broke off, and Pelleter realized that he
was glaring at the young man.

Martin swallowed, but to his credit did not look away.
"I just wanted to know if you could tell."

Pelleter tried to relax his pose. The Mahossier business had been big news at the time of the killings and was
perhaps not as forgotten as Pelleter sometimes hoped.
Officer Martin was just the right age that he had no
doubt followed the story avidly, perhaps even deciding to

become a police officer because of it. And now here was Pelleter, and there was a murder to be solved.

Pelleter shook his head, trying to soften his expression. "You never can tell. Later, afterwards, of course, and then you wonder if you always knew." He considered his words. "Men are capable of anything."

This upset Martin. "But what Mahossier did, I mean—"

Pelleter put a hand on the young man's shoulder wishing he could honestly relieve his anguish.

Martin said, "I just want to be ready."

"If you saw the man now, you would know," Pelleter reassured him, which of course was not quite the same as knowing in advance.

Martin was slightly relieved, and Pelleter forced a close-mouthed smile, thinking of the power Mahossier wielded now because people knew what he had done. He tried to remember the first time he interviewed Mahossier, when he was just a suspect, if he had known then. He really couldn't say.

Letreau slammed the phone down in his office, drawing everyone's attention. He was breathing heavily, trying to get control of himself.

The phone on the counter rang and Pelleter picked up. "Yes…Chief Inspector Pelleter…I need you to pull the file on a Marcel Meranger…All known associates, family, friends, accomplices, enemies, anyone…How long will it take…Good, then I'll wait…"

Letreau came out of his office. His face was red, but he otherwise seemed to be under control. He watched Pelleter on the phone.

Pelleter said, "Wait…Actually I'm going to put another

officer on, you give the information to him…He'll wait for it…Thank you." Pelleter handed the phone to Martin. "Write down everything he tells you."

When Pelleter turned to Letreau, the chief of police's face went a deeper shade of red before he even started talking. "Fournier said he'd look into it."

"I see."

"I could—"

Pelleter stepped forward and took Letreau by the arm, leading him towards his office. All eyes were on the two senior men. Once in the office, Pelleter closed the door, and then stood watching Letreau pace once again, working himself up over the situation.

Letreau stopped and looked at his friend. "I'm sorry. We haven't had an unsolved homicide in this town in thirty years."

"You don't have one yet."

"Fournier said that he would look into whether or not they were missing a prisoner, but that he thought he would know by now if the man had been missing over twenty-four hours."

"He should. Did you say we would come down there?"

"He said that wasn't necessary, because he'd be tied up trying to find out what happened and the warden, of course, isn't there, so if we want to, we should come tomorrow. I told him that perhaps the warden would want to know about this. He said there was no way to get in touch with the warden at the moment, but that he would have everything under control, and that if we felt it was necessary, we could come tomorrow."

From the outside, it was impossible to read Pelleter's

expression, it appeared to be so calm, but in fact, he felt exactly the same way as Chief Letreau.

"I could kill that man Fournier. He's so cool. It's not natural," Letreau said.

Pelleter had thought the same thing earlier in the day. The man acted as though nothing could surprise him. And the warden rushing out of town like that was a bit convenient too.

Letreau said, "I guess I'm going to go see Benoît again. Take a look at his basement."

"The baker?"

"I need to do something, damn it!" And Letreau went red once again. "We didn't know it was a murder when we saw him this morning. Maybe we missed something."

Letreau went to the hook behind the door to retrieve his overcoat. He pulled open the door. An old woman stood in the public space of the station holding a small soaked dog under her right arm as though it were a handbag. A young man who had not removed his hat was standing next to her, and they were both talking at the same time to the two police officers who normally occupied the desks. The noise of the argument filled the small space of the station, creating an increased sense of tension. Martin was still on the phone, his left hand pressed against his free ear.

Letreau crossed the station, ignoring the scene. Nearly at the door, he said to Pelleter, "Are you coming with me?"

Pelleter said, "Go ahead."

Letreau went out, the sound of the rain momentarily blending in with the noise of the argument before the door slammed shut.

Pelleter sat down in one of the waiting room chairs watching the scene. There was nothing to do but wait.

The officers managed to get the two parties separated, and the story unfolded that the young man had nearly hit the old lady's dog with his car as he parked it on the square. The young man claimed that the dog had been in the street. Nobody was hurt.

Pelleter wondered what it would be like to be a policeman in such a town. The weather had everyone on edge.

"Chief Inspector!"

It was Martin at the counter. He had hung up the phone. Pelleter went up to him. "Got anything?"

The young officer handed over a list in the now familiar handwriting. "Here's the list. It's a long one." He was proud of his work, and watched Pelleter expectantly as the inspector scanned the names.

There were at least ninety names on the paper written in small even lines. It was a lot of names to go through, but it could be done if it had to be. Pelleter scanned the list and recognized a few of them from many years ago, but for the most part they meant nothing to him. Many of them were probably also in prison or dead.

"Chief Inspector," Martin said, and he stood up from his stool to lean over the counter. He pointed to a name on the top of the list. "I thought I recognized that name," he said.

The name was Clotilde-ma-Fleur Meranger, and a note beside the name identified her as the dead man's daughter.

"It's such an unusual first name, I figured how many people could there be? So I had the person on the phone look up whether or not Mademoiselle Meranger had since been married, and it turns out she is. She's married to Shem Rosenkrantz, the American writer. She's now Clotilde-ma-Fleur Rosenkrantz."

The woman with the wet dog had been appeased, and the group was now talking jocularly in more normal tones.

Martin waited for a reaction from Pelleter, and then he said, "They live here in town."

Pelleter registered this new piece of information. Meranger's daughter lived in town. If anyone knew anything about this, it would be the daughter.

"Where?"

The Rosenkrantz home was on the western edge of town on the Rue Principale where the houses were spaced further apart before giving way wholly to farmland. It was a small two-story wooden house painted a faint olive green with white shutters. The low fence surrounding the property was more decorative than anything.

The rain was holding steady, but Pelleter had refused a ride to the house, preferring to see the town on foot. The baker's house where the body had been found was in another quarter of the town, to the north, but that didn't mean anything. The town was not very large. Meranger could have been on his way to see his daughter, or he could have already been there. And there was still the matter of who had helped him out of the prison, and who would want to.

Pelleter let himself in through the front gate. The house was well maintained, and somehow managed to look cheery even in the rain. At the door, shielded by the overhang, the remaining water streamed off his hat and coat before settling to a steady drip. There were no lights at the front of the house, but he could see that there were some lit towards the rear. He knocked.

A car passed in the street, on its way to town, not yet slowing its country pace.

There was no response from the house. Pelleter knocked again, looking up and around him as if he could gauge if the house was empty.

It was possible that the Rosenkrantzes were out, although in this rain it seemed unlikely. And Pelleter thought they would not have left any lights burning if that were the case. He was thankful for the overhang, but he was growing tired of the sound of the rain, of the weight of his coat, of the clammy feeling of the weather in general.

He knocked again with great force and the door shuddered a little in its frame.

A figure appeared from the back of the house, a silhouette blocking the light, visible through the window in the door. The man came up to the door with quick strides, and pulled it open violently. "What do you want?"

He was about Pelleter's age. His French was almost unaccented, but something still gave him away as a foreigner. Perhaps it was his manner.

Pelleter showed his papers. "Is Madame Rosenkrantz at home?"

"No. What's it about?"

"I'd like to speak to her directly."

"Well, she's not here. And I'm trying to work. So sorry." He made no motion to close the door, but by his stance it was clear that he was about to.

"It's about her father. I think she would want to speak to me."

The man's stance opened up, and he took a step so that he was standing at the threshold of the door. "If it's about her father, then she definitely doesn't want to speak to you. She's done with him. Finished. She hates his guts."

"That doesn't change that I need to speak to her."

The man repositioned himself, as if readying for a confrontation. He was a broad man, of a similar build to Pelleter. He had not let himself get soft with age or with the comfort of working at a typewriter. "My wife doesn't talk to her father and hasn't for thirteen years. So anything she has to say, I can say right now, which is nothing. You got that?"

Pelleter didn't answer.

Monsieur Rosenkrantz backed up. "Now I'm working." He started to close the door.

Pelleter turned slightly as if to go, and then turned back just as the door was almost shut, Rosenkrantz still visible through the window. "One more thing. If your wife no longer talks to her father, then why did she choose to live in the town closest to his prison?"

Rosenkrantz jerked the door back open, and stood glaring at Pelleter as though he were going to start a fight. Instead he slammed the door without answering, and stormed off into the back of the house, disappearing in the low light.

Pelleter found the stump of his cigar in his pocket and put it in his mouth. He chewed it first in the left corner of his mouth and then shifted it with his tongue to the right corner. It was too wet out to light a new cigar, so the stump would do for the walk back into town.

He stepped down from out of the protection of the overhang, walked the length of the path, and out through the gate.

The storm brought an early evening. As he walked through town, many windows were lit, but their lights didn't extend far beyond the panes of glass. Benoît's bakery was closed; it kept early hours. The café where he and Letreau had eaten breakfast was lit and filled with evening patrons stopping for a drink before heading home, or having an early dinner. At the edges of the streets, the rainwater was above the cobblestones as it gushed towards the sewer entrances.

Pelleter could have returned to the station, but there was little to report and most likely even less to learn. It also would have made it harder to refuse Letreau's offer of dinner. He didn't want the conversation or the comfort. He turned instead to his hotel, the Verargent, at the northeast corner of the square.

He left instructions at the desk that he would be down for his dinner in one hour and he asked to have a toddy sent up to the room.

Upstairs, he peeled off his coat and hat, retrieved a fresh cigar and lit it and then picked up the phone.

"Get me the police station…Yes." He hung up.

He sat at the edge of the bed, smoking. The phone rang. It was Letreau.

"Yes…No, nothing…She wasn't there…I didn't expect as much…No, I'm going to stay in the hotel tonight. My apologies…We'll meet in the café in the morning and go to the prison…Good. Goodnight…Call if you need to."

He hung up. The world outside was invisible from the bed, the window a black mirror, but the sound of the rain trickled in, interrupted occasionally by the sound of a motor.

It bothered him that Mahossier had said somebody was killing prisoners and then the dead man in town turned out to be a prisoner.

And the American writer had seemed awfully argumentative, but perhaps if your father-in-law was in prison it would be the cause of some anger. People reacted differently to the police anyway.

A girl brought him his toddy, and he dressed for dinner while he drank. The warm drink, the smoke from his cigar, and the dry clothes made him feel a new man, and he realized that he was hungry. He pushed aside the questions of the day, and went down to dinner in an optimistic mood.

The girl who had brought him his drink was behind the counter reading a magazine. The dining room, just off of the lobby, was a small ill-lit room with six round tables fit close together. There was only one other guest there, at a table in the far corner. Pelleter took one of the smaller tables near the window to benefit from the wall sconce. He could feel the outside cold seeping through the glass windowpanes.

The hotel owner appeared through a door in the back. He clapped his hands together and spoke in a loud voice while still across the room. "Inspector! Your dinner's coming right away. It's finished right now. The girl will bring it. Some weather, no?"

The other guest turned from his meal at this performance. He and Pelleter exchanged an embarrassed, apologetic look, and then the man returned to his meal.

The owner was standing over Pelleter now.

"You must tell me all about this business," the owner said. "A man killed in the streets? In Verargent? No, no, no, no, no." He clucked his tongue and shook his head.

Pelleter's good mood soured. It was inevitable in a small town that these things would be discussed, but it was not preferable. "We don't know," he said.

"But Benoît found him in the street, the poor man!"

The girl appeared with the meal, chicken in a wine sauce with sautéed asparagus on the side. She set the plate, which was still steaming, in front of Pelleter and stood behind the owner.

"Ah, here it is. You will love it. A personal specialty. *Bon appetit*." He turned to the girl, and shooed her away. "Leave the inspector alone. Go, go." He turned back, and opened his mouth just as Pelleter put the first bite of chicken into his own. Then he must have realized that he too was pestering the inspector, because he said "*Bon appetit*" again and turned to leave, stopping at the other guest's table before disappearing into the back.

The food was good, but Pelleter ate mechanically, without tasting it. The owner's inquiries had once again turned his mind back to the matter at hand. Who had gotten Meranger out of prison, and was he dead before or after?

Halfway through his meal, a young woman appeared

in the entryway to the dining room. She was very pretty in a delicate way. She wore an expensive dress, which accentuated her slight form, but it was clear that she was not comfortable in it and used her shawl to cover herself. She stood just inside the entrance looking into the dinning room, turning her wedding ring on her finger with her right hand.

Pelleter waited to let her make up her own mind, and then he waved her in.

She fell forward as though she had been released from someone's grip, and rushed across the dining room to his table. "Chief Inspector, I am so sorry to disturb you."

The other guest turned again at the sound of her voice. In such a small town, there was never any privacy, always somebody close at hand. And yet no one had seen or heard a thing the night before when Meranger had been murdered.

Pelleter indicated the chair across from him, and she pulled it out far enough that she could sit at the edge of the seat, not quite committing herself to staying.

"I am Madame Rosenkrantz," she said, and then looked down at her hands in her lap as though this were something shameful.

"Yes," Pelleter said. She was younger than he had expected—this girl was no more than nineteen. He could see why Rosenkrantz had married her. She was charming to look at.

She looked up at him. "My husband said that you came to see me."

"And he let you come out to find me at this time of night in this weather?"

"He was not happy. But in the end he does what I tell him to do." She looked down again at this confession.

Pelleter tried to imagine the American writer taking orders from a woman, and he saw that it might be possible. "I'm surprised he even told you I had come. He wasn't happy to see me."

"That's just because you caught him when he was working. He's a different person when he writes. That's why I often go out."

"Where?"

"Just out," she said, and left it at that, her gaze fixed on him, some of her shyness gone. "He said you came about my father."

"Yes."

She waited for him to say more, but when he didn't, she said, "He's dead, isn't he?"

"Yes."

She looked down again, and he could tell she was twirling her ring by the movement of her arms. He watched for any change in her expression, but there was nothing, no tears, no surprise. "Murdered?" she said, her voice soft but firm.

"How did you know?" Pelleter said, eager.

"This man the baker found, and then you arriving…" She looked up. "What else could it be?" And with that a nervous smile sought to hide any other feelings.

"Your husband said that you hated your father. That you hadn't spoken to him since he'd gone to prison. He was very emphatic."

"Please, please eat," she said, indicating his food. "I've interrupted your meal."

"Why did you hate your father?"

"I didn't."

"You don't seem very upset over his death."

"He was dead to me already. But I didn't hate him. He was still my father." She shrugged. "He killed my mother."

Pelleter was surprised. "That's not in his record."

"Well he did." She pursed her lips. "He didn't kill her directly. He put her in danger, and she was killed. He owed money. He ran away." She shrugged again. "That's how these things work."

Pelleter looked at her again. He saw now that her initial shyness was a product of her current luck, the unexpected wealth of her husband, and her newfound domestic happiness. She was not a stranger to a rougher life. It had probably served her well to remain unnoticed in that life as well, and that would not have been easy as pretty as she was.

"I should think your husband is now a father to you."

"Because of my age? No, not at all. We're—"

"Why would someone have wanted to kill your father?"

"He was a bad man," she said.

"But you can think of no specific reason? There was no one in particular who would have wanted him dead?"

She shook her head, flustered again by his insistence. "No…I don't know…I had nothing to do with my father."

He pressed on. "But you went to see him."

She looked down once more. "Yes," she said.

"Your husband didn't know that."

"No…I don't think so."

"Why not tell him?"

She didn't answer.

"If it needed to be kept a secret, why go see your father at all?"

She looked at him, and her expression was strong. "Because he was my father," she said.

"When did you see him last?"

"I don't know. A month ago. Maybe more. I didn't go regularly. Sometimes a whole year or more…"

"Did he say anything? Was he afraid? Did he talk of being together again soon, of getting out of prison?"

"No. Nothing. We didn't talk long. Somebody had been killed that week in the prison, but that happens. It was nothing…I never stayed long…Once I was there, I could never figure out why."

Pelleter watched her. She looked at her hands fidgeting in her lap, then up at him defiantly, then back at her hands, in a cycle. He thought of the American writer, of his bluster. "Tell me," he said suddenly.

She looked at him in panic. "There's nothing! That's it!"

He slammed his hands on the table in fists, rattling the china. "Tell me!"

"There's nothing! My father's dead, I just wanted to be sure. That's all!"

They stared at each other, neither looking away, neither backing down.

At last Pelleter said, "Well, he's dead." He picked up his silverware and resumed eating. The food was cold now. It made no difference.

Madame Rosenkrantz gathered herself, taking a deep breath, and then got up. She stood over him for a moment, watching him eat. Then she said, "Are you going to do something about this?"

He looked up at her, watching her carefully for a reaction. "Do you care?"

There was no reaction. "Yes," she said.

He looked back at his plate. "I am."

She left, taking strong steps across the dining room, but pausing in the lobby, once again appearing like a lost young girl.

The dining room was quiet. The rain had stopped.

Upstairs, the other diner was just stepping out of the door to the room across the hall from Pelleter's. He stopped short at the sight of the inspector, and then tried on an ingratiating smile, extending his hand as he stepped up to meet Pelleter halfway down the hall.

"Inspector Pelleter!"

The man took Pelleter's hand almost against his will and pumped it, blocking the inspector's path.

"I don't mean any familiarity. I couldn't help but hear some of the conversation downstairs. It's very exciting to meet a celebrity."

Pelleter freed his hand and tried to step around the man. "A pleasure," he said.

"Could I ask you a few questions? I hate to be an imposition, but you read things in the papers and you're never able to tell if they've gotten it quite right. Like our own local celebrity, Mahossier."

The man had placed himself in such a way that Pelleter could not pass him without force.

"Is it true that he kept the children in cages?"

Pelleter felt tired. Was there not enough sadness in the world that people had to revel in the worst of it?

"I remember reading that you found a child in a cage, and that there were other small cages next to it...And that he had dug a pit in his basement where he would force the children to fight each other if they wanted to be fed...An image like that stays with you. I still have nightmares about it, and that's just from reading the stories. Is it true?"

"Excuse me," Pelleter said, but he made no attempt to get by.

"I just don't understand how somebody could do that, how it works. He would kidnap the children, and then starve them..."

The man paused, observing Pelleter with a keen eye, as though he were testing him, to see the effect of this story.

"Meanwhile, he would have two of the already starving children fight each other to set an example. Am I getting this right?"

All these years later and people were still talking about this monster. He should be forgotten, not famous.

The man went on. "Yes. Then the children would fight to the death, and the winner was allowed to eat the other children's carcasses, locked away until the next battle. Amazing."

"Why are you so interested?" Pelleter said, determined to give no signs one way or the other.

"Oh, just curiosity, curiosity. I have an amateur interest in the mystery of crime, let's say."

Pelleter felt his anger rising. "Excuse me," he said again.

"Oh, of course, it's getting late. But just tell me, is that really true? Surely the newspapers must have exaggerated. No one would do that to children just for his own entertainment."

"I have nothing more to say on this. It was a long time ago."

"Then maybe you could tell me about our local murder. Have you any suspects there?"

Pelleter took a step forward as though to walk through the man.

The man held his ground so that he was too close, directly in Pelleter's face. "I don't believe that anyone could get away with what Mahossier did even if he would do it. You have to tell me that. It can't be that that is how it was."

It was as though the man needed some reaction out of Pelleter, as though he were deliberately pushing him to see what kind of a man he was.

"There were really bones with children's teeth marks on them? That detail always seemed too extreme."

Pelleter grabbed the man's shoulder then and pushed him out of the way. The man fell against the wall, and hopped to regain his balance as Pelleter stepped around him. "There's nothing more to be said."

The man called at Pelleter's back, "So it really is true, and you saw all of that. Why didn't you kill him on sight?"

Pelleter turned back and rushed the man, stopping inches away from his face. "Because that's not how the law works."

"When there are murdered men in the streets of Ver-argent, maybe the law doesn't work."

Pelleter glared at the man. He could have told the man of the years of scars on the surviving boy, the evidence of many battles fought and won. That the bite marks on the bones suggested that this last boy had killed no less than six other children in his short life, and that he was still in an institution in the city unable to talk, often in restraints. They had managed to keep that out of the papers, for the boy's sake.

Instead he said, "Good night," and turned away.

Behind him the man said, "I didn't mean anything by it. I just wanted to know."

Pelleter unlocked his door.

"You—"

But the man stopped himself before Pelleter had even closed the door.

In the room, the inspector felt too wound up for such a small place. Mahossier was one case. He could have told the man of so many other cases over the years that the papers were too busy to notice. Was one horror really more terrible than another when somebody was dead?

And somebody was dead again, and Mahossier was close at hand again. Even if Mahossier had nothing to do with this, it just made Pelleter uncomfortable.

He took a deep breath and let it out slowly. It had just been a tactless man. As he had told Officer Martin that afternoon, people can do anything. Right now, only the questions were important:

Who moved the body?

Why hide that Meranger was a prisoner by changing his clothes?

He shrugged off his jacket and stepped over to the bed. He tried to review his interview with Madame Rosenkrantz as he sank onto the mattress.

Instead, the image of that lone boy in a cage in Mahossier's basement crowded everything else out. His anger flared up again at the guest from across the hall, and he clenched his fists and ground his teeth.

Of course the papers had left out the smell. Mahossier's basement had smelled like a latrine outside a slaughterhouse. Pelleter had had to discard the suit he wore that day, because the smell had woven its way into the cloth.

These were the memories that he had to fight against when he saw that clownish glee on Mahossier's face in the interrogation room at Malniveau. There he had succeeded in being all business. And now some curious civilian threw him off his guard.

He looked at the phone sitting in the pool of light from the bedside lamp. He checked his watch.

It was too late. If he called Madame Pelleter now it would only make her worry.

## 4. Another One

The next day was clear as Pelleter and Letreau set out for Malniveau Prison. The fields were muddy and there were occasional twin stripes of tire tracks on the pavement from where trucks and automobiles had turned onto the main road from unpaved country roads.

Fournier met them himself at the front entrance. He wore a tailored gray suit that looked as though it had been pressed that morning. He had a clipboard in hand, and began to speak before Remy had managed to relock the front door.

"Meranger was present at roll call two nights ago, April 4... The guard who took roll call yesterday morning counted him as present...There was no exercise yesterday because of the rain, so the next roll call would have been last night, and you contacted me before then."

"Where's the guard who made the mistake?" Pelleter said.

"He's already been reprimanded."

"I still want to talk with him."

"It will not happen again...I have long suggested to the warden that certain reformations must be made to our roll call procedures." His manner was sharp and authoritative. He was not going to be pushed around in his own domain.

Pelleter and Letreau locked eyes. Fournier was impossible.

Letreau said, "We're all in this mess together."

Fournier opened the door to the administrative offices. "The Meranger file—"

"I'd like to see Meranger's cell," Pelleter said.

Fournier looked back at him, still holding the office door. "We have been through the cell," he said flatly. "There's nothing to see."

Suddenly Inspector Pelleter stepped so close to Fournier that the two men's coats were almost touching. "I am trying to do my job. Your job is to assist me in doing my job. So I don't care if you've reprimanded your guard or if you've searched the cell or if you think you've got everything under control. I want you to help me when I say help me and otherwise I want you to stay out of my way."

Fournier's face remained impassive during this speech, but when it was clear that Pelleter was done, he looked away first. "Right. He was on cell block D, which is on the second floor."

Pelleter stepped back. Fournier pushed past him and led the way through a door at the end of the hall, only several doors down from the room in which Pelleter had met with Mahossier the day before. It opened onto a set of stone stairs. There was a cloying smell of mildew, and the temperature was noticeably cooler than it had been in the hall.

Fournier seemed to have recovered from his dressing-down, and was using the opportunity to proudly show off the prison. "The doors lock behind us as we go, so that anyone caught without a key at any juncture would be trapped until somebody else came through…We've of course never had a successful escape here, and there hasn't even been an attempt since the war."

"Until now," Pelleter said.

"Well, we'll see."

"What do you mean?"

"The man was dead, after all."

They reached the second-floor landing, and Fournier sorted through his keys. "You'll notice the two doors. The one to the left here leads to the inside hallway between the cells, and the one further to the right," he said stepping over to it, "leads to the outside gallery that overlooks the inner courtyard." He fit his key into the outer door. "You'll want to look at this…The prisoners weren't able to go out yesterday because of the rain, so they were eager to go out today."

He opened the door, and a breeze rushed in, blowing cold air. They stepped out onto the gallery, a narrow iron walkway only wide enough for one man. A guard stood ten paces away, carrying a shotgun.

The prisoners were in the courtyard below. Many held their arms across their chests against the cold. They were like the random crowd on a market day, jostling against one another, walking with little regard as to where they were going.

"The guards down there carry no firearms." Fournier pointed out the other guards along the gallery. "The men up here have shotguns…The prisoners that are allowed outside get one hour in the morning and one hour in the afternoon."

"Did Meranger have outdoor privileges?"

"Yes. He was a model prisoner. He'd been here a long time."

Pelleter watched the prisoners milling about in the relative freedom of the yard.

Suddenly a cry came from the far corner. Everyone's attention was drawn to the sound, and immediately the prisoners were shouting and rushing into the area.

The guards on the ground began to run as well, joining the general melee.

Fournier turned back to the door, shuffling through his keys. His movements hurried but precise. He went through the door, leaving Pelleter and Letreau locked out on the gallery with the armed guards.

As they watched, the guards on the ground got to the center of the crowd, and forced the prisoners back. A prisoner was lying on the ground, his hands clutching at something on his chest.

"They've knifed him," Letreau said.

The man's mouth was wide open in agony.

Fournier appeared below them. He cut across the yard, directly into the crowd, yelling at the prisoners as he went.

The guards on the gallery had their rifles in hand, and watched with care.

Two men appeared with a stretcher through one of the doors. The prisoners parted to let them through. The noise had diminished enough that the injured man's cries could be made out as he rolled on the ground.

Fournier was at the center of the crowd, yelling at prisoners. He grabbed one man and pushed him back.

The injured man was moved onto the stretcher, and rushed inside.

Fournier, still yelling at the prisoners, followed.

By the time the prison yard was emptied and one of the guards could readmit them into the building, Pelleter and Letreau were thoroughly chilled. The guard who escorted them to the infirmary talked continuously, still energized from the excitement of the stabbing.

"You sure saw something…It can be so dull out here, just standing for hours and hours at a time. You forget that these are dangerous criminals. You almost let your guard down…Then, pow! It's a powder keg…You don't know if you should shoot or not."

Every door they came to required two sets of keys. There were locked guard boxes at all major intersections. The guard had to return his shotgun to the armory, a locked room in which the guns were locked in cages and overseen by the arms keeper.

"How often does something like this happen?"

"It could be months. When I first started here, there was a whole year before anything happened. I didn't believe the older guys who said different. But this month! Wow! There must be some kind of gang war going on. Here we are."

Pelleter stopped him outside of the infirmary. "How many?"

The guard rocked on his feet, he was so excited. "I don't know, four, five. The guards don't always find out about everything, you know?"

"Any dead?"

"Not that I know of."

Pelleter nodded at that, as if all of the answers had been expected. He pushed his way into the infirmary.

It was a small white room with six beds, three on each side of the room. The knifed man was in the furthest bed on the right. His shirt had been cut off, and two guards and a nurse were holding him down as the doctor stitched the wound on his chest and stomach. The man did not seem to be struggling.

"He's been given morphine," Fournier said from just inside the door. He was taking notes on his clipboard. "He'll live. It's only a gash."

"Can we talk to him?"

"He doesn't know who did it. He was walking and then he was on the ground in pain. It could be any number of people who were in his vicinity, but he's not even sure who was nearby."

"Any enemies? Did he have a fight with someone?"

Fournier held his pencil against his clipboard with a snap. "No. Nothing. I asked him."

"Would he tell you?"

Fournier's nostrils flared, and his movements were sharper than usual, the only indication that he was under a great deal of stress. "Listen, Inspector. If we're all in this together, then you're just going to have to trust me. He didn't see anything. He doesn't know who did it. That's it."

A moan came from the prisoner. The doctor could be heard placating him. They were almost finished.

"Now if you still need to see Meranger's cell, let's go and be fast about it. I have a lot of work to do. We've got to search all of the prisoners and all of the cells. Not that we'll find anything, but it has to be done."

Pelleter would have liked to question the prisoner himself, but he had seen the incident and it was quite possible that the man knew nothing. It could wait.

"Yes, let's," Pelleter said, and he stepped back as if to let Fournier pass. Then he stopped him. "And what does the warden say of all of these stabbings?"

"All of them?"

"The guard said that there have been at least four this month."

Fournier's brow furrowed, his eyes narrowing. "If you count Meranger then this is three that I know of, and for all we know Meranger was stabbed on the outside."

Letreau started to speak, but Pelleter held up a hand to hold him off. "Surely, you will be calling the warden about this?" Pelleter said.

"The warden has left me in charge because I am fully capable of being in charge. He will be informed when he returns on Monday. No need to ruin his vacation."

"Of course."

Fournier nodded his head once for emphasis, then led out the door.

Letreau stepped in close to Pelleter. "What's going on?"

"There's been a stabbing."

"I know there's been a stabbing, but…"

"Then you know what I know."

Fournier had gotten ahead of them, and he waited at the next door for the two of them to catch up. In the hallways, away from the courtyard, with no one in sight but the occasional guard, it was impossible to know that a man had almost been killed within these walls less than an hour before. The stones were gray and impassive.

Meranger's jail cell was on the outer wall, with a narrow window that looked out onto the neighboring fields. The space was large enough for the iron cot and steel toilet with barely enough room left over to stand. Fournier stood impatiently in the hallway, reviewing the papers on his clipboard, and Letreau stood outside the cell door watching Pelleter survey the room.

Meranger's few possessions had been dumped into a box on the bed from when Fournier had made his own investigation. There were three books—a bible and two mystery novels—a travel chess set, odd-shaped stones most likely found in the yard below, a dried flower, and a small bundle of letters tied with a string.

The letters were all in the same feminine hand, although it had grown more assured over the years. There were four letters in total. The most recent letter was from only two months prior:

> *Father,*
>     *It's unfair of you to be so demanding. You don't know what it costs me to make those visits or to even write these letters. Every time I tell myself that this will be the last, that I can not take it anymore. I remind myself of what you have done and all the reasons I have to hate you, and I make new resolutions. But I still fear you, and I still wish to please you, and all I end up doing is reprimanding myself.*

*You must believe though that my husband would be enraged if you were to contact me or even if he knew that I contacted you. He treats me like a dream, but he can still be a rash man.*

*I will not promise to visit you again or even to write, but you must know that you are in my thoughts. And I will be here in Verargent when you are on the outside. You shall see. As you said, your little girl is all grown up now already.*

*Clotilde-ma-Fleur*

The other letters were much the same. A photograph had been inserted in one of them, of a couple standing with a young girl. The woman looked much like Madame Rosenkrantz, and Pelleter figured that it was Clotilde-ma-Fleur's mother.

He refolded the letters along their much-folded creases, and put them back into the box. He bent down and checked beneath the bed, beneath the toilet, and ran his hands along the walls. Then he stepped out of the cell. "Right," he said. "It was as you said."

Fournier looked up from his clipboard. "Of course," he said.

Letreau tried to catch Pelleter's eye, but Pelleter put on an air of one who was wasting his time and was ready to leave.

Fournier started to lead them back the way they had come, but they hadn't gone two steps when a voice said, "Hello, Pelleter."

The three men stopped, and Pelleter looked at the door to the cell beside the one they had just been in. A smiling face was visible in the small window in the door.

"How is Madame Pelleter?"

It was Meranger's neighbor: Mahossier.

In the police car in front of the prison, Letreau turned to Pelleter before starting the engine. "Can you tell me what's going on?"

Pelleter stared straight ahead at the prison walls. The sun had come up fully, and now, with the last traces of the rain burned away, even the prison appeared gayer in the light. "Was Meranger slashed or stabbed?" Pelleter said.

"Stabbed. More than once."

Letreau waited, but the inspector remained silent.

"Pelleter, talk to me. I appreciate that you've chosen to help, but this is still my responsibility."

"Start the car. We should get back to town. It's time to eat."

Letreau sighed and started the car. The pavement on the road had dried to a slate gray. Puddles of rainwater in the fields reflected the sun, little patches of light dotting the fields.

Pelleter pulled a cheap oilcloth-covered notebook from his pocket and flipped it open. "This is what we know… *Tuesday, April 4, just after eight PM: A man is found dead in the gutter by Monsieur Benoît outside of his house. At first it is believed that he drowned in rainwater while drunk, but it is later discovered that he had been stabbed several times and then had his clothing changed to hide the wounds.*"

"Or to hide that he was a prisoner. He would have been wearing his grays."

Pelleter went on: "*Wednesday morning the murderer Mahossier claims that the prisoners at Malniveau are being systematically murdered, and that he doesn't feel safe.*"

"Wait a second."

"*The dead man turns out to be Marcel Meranger, a prisoner at Malniveau Prison.*"

"Wait one second. Is that what Mahossier told you? Then do you think that this Meranger murder is tied up in something larger?"

"I don't think anything. This is just what we know. *Wednesday night Meranger's daughter Madame Rosenkrantz says that she knows nothing about her father's murder. She claims at first to have nothing to do with him, then to have visited him on occasion. Her letters are found in Meranger's cell.*

"*Thursday morning another prisoner is knifed at the prison… Nobody can agree on the number of prisoners stabbed or killed in the last month.*" Pelleter closed his notebook and put it away. "And that's it, which is nothing." He said it with the bitterness of a man who has failed at a simple task.

"Somebody had to have gotten Meranger out of prison whether it was before or after he was killed. If we could figure that out, then we might know a lot more."

Pelleter didn't answer. Instead he reached into his pocket, retrieved his cigar, and smoked in a restless silence without enjoying it.

Suddenly, he said, "What do you think of Fournier?"

Letreau shifted in his seat. "You know what I think of Fournier. I could wring his neck. Although really until today, I didn't know anything about him. He's only been here a few months. He came from another prison, and the word was that he is extremely good at what he does... But I don't know. The prison really is its own entity."

"You said the men who work there live in town," Pelleter said.

"It's as if there's a wall of silence somewhere along this road. Sometimes things get said, and others..." He shrugged. "If only the warden were here. This Fournier seems intent on blocking us out at every step. That's what I think."

"And the warden?"

"He's brutish and controlling. He started at the bottom, so administration might not be his forte, but he's been there forever, and the prison gets run."

Pelleter nodded, considering this.

"What are you thinking? That the staff has something to do with all of this? These are prison stabbings. They happen. This wouldn't even be our problem if it wasn't for this body in town."

"I'm not thinking anything. I'm just trying to understand. What can you tell me about the American author? Do you think he would have killed his father-in-law?"

"Rosenkrantz? He keeps to himself mostly. That's why he chose to move out here, as far as I understand. He was part of the American scene in the city for many years, getting his photograph taken at bars, drinking until sunrise. He produces a book every year or two, and they're apparently big sellers back in the States. He can seem loud, but I always figured that's because he's American. Clotilde caused him to settle down. She means everything to him."

"Enough to kill for."

"I don't know. Somehow I doubt it."

"Why?"

"He's all bark and no bite."

"So we still know nothing."

"We know that one man's dead," Letreau said. "There's that."

"There's that," Pelleter said like it was a curse.

The mud-drenched fields made the whole countryside appear dirty.

Letreau looked over at the inspector, but Pelleter was lost deep in thought again, a scowl on his face.

The town had come alive in the sunshine. There seemed to be an impossible number of people on the streets, hurrying from shop to shop, sitting out in the center of the square along the base of the war monument. The café where Pelleter took lunch had every seat filled, and the inspector had to sit on one of three stools at the counter.

Letreau had returned to the station in order to see about his other duties.

Pelleter ate with his back to the crowd. Occasionally he would hear the name Benoît, and he knew that the town was discussing the murder, but the tone was of idle gossip, with little regard for the reality of the crime.

The man beside him pushed his plate back, and stood up, and another man took the seat immediately.

"Inspector Pelleter?" the man said. He sat sideways on the seat and had a notebook and pencil in hand. "Philippe Servières, reporter with the *Verargent Vérité*.

Could I ask you a few questions about the Meranger
murder?"

"No," Pelleter said without looking at the man.

"What about what you're doing in town? You arrived
before the body was discovered. Was there another matter
you were investigating?"

Pelleter drank from his glass and then pushed back his
plate.

"I know that you and Chief Letreau have made two
trips to the prison already, and that the warden has left
town. This sounds like something that's bigger than just
Verargent. Malniveau is a national prison after all. The
people have a right to know."

Pelleter stood up, turned to the reporter, and stopped
short. It was the man from the hallway last night.

"You…"

The man flinched as though the inspector had made a
move to hit him. "I had to try," he said.

"Try what?" Pelleter growled.

"If you would talk about an old case, even out of anger,
maybe you would talk about the new case too."

The man was a small-town reporter, practically an
amateur. He mistook Pelleter for an amateur too. "I know
you're doing your job, but you better let me do mine."

Pelleter called the proprietor over and settled his bill.

The reporter stood too. "I'm going to write this story
for a special evening edition either way. You might as well
get your say in it."

Pelleter gave him one last look, which silenced him,
and then the inspector went out into the street.

He crossed the square. People went about their daily

business. It was as Letreau had said: the town seemed unaware that twenty miles away there was another community where somebody had just been attacked that morning. The newspaperman hadn't even mentioned the knifing.

He turned the corner at Town Hall to go to the police station, and as he did a figure jumped out from between two of the police cars parked at the curb and rushed Pelleter.

Pelleter turned to face his attacker, and was able to register the face just in time to not draw his weapon.

"I warned you, damn it!" Monsieur Rosenkrantz said, forcing Pelleter back against the wall without touching him. His face was red, and he leaned forward, crowding Pelleter, his chest and shoulders pushed out.

Pelleter watched the American writer for any signs that he would actually turn violent. He remembered that Letreau had said all bark and no bite.

"I told you to stay away from her. That she had nothing to say."

"She came to me," Pelleter said.

"I told you!" Rosenkrantz leaned even further forward, and then he pulled himself away, spinning in place and punching the air. "Damn it!" he said in English. Then he turned back to Pelleter, and said in French, "She didn't come home last night. Clotilde is missing."

## 5. Five Wooden Boxes

Pelleter watched the American writer pace the sidewalk in front of him, full of nervous energy. The inspector stayed on his guard, but it soon became clear that Rosenkrantz's violence, like at the house the day before, was entirely auditory. There was no danger.

"Come, let's go inside," Pelleter said.

Rosenkrantz shook his head. "I've been looking for you. They won't let me make a report anyway, it's too soon."

"Has she ever run away before?"

Rosenkrantz jerked towards him. "She hasn't run away." Then his manner eased again. "When she got home yesterday from her shopping, I told her that you had come around…She insisted on going to see you. She was in a panic. She was convinced that her father must be dead."

Pelleter nodded.

"I know now that he is, but then…Well, good, I hated the man for all that he put Clotilde through as a girl, for what he did to her mother. He deserved to die. I hope he suffered…But last night, I told Clotilde to not get involved…That it only ever upset her, and that she should stay home…It was raining still…But she went out anyway."

"I saw her."

"Was she upset?"

"I wouldn't say that."

Rosenkrantz shook his head. "That's Clotilde. You can't always know."

"Does she have friends she would stay with? The hotel?"

"I checked. Both. No one has seen her."

The two men looked at each other. Neither said what they were both thinking, that it would be easy for her to have gotten on the train and to be almost anywhere by now.

"Do you think that she hated her father?" Pelleter asked.

"If you're suggesting that Clotilde might have killed the old man, you can forget it. She can't kill a fly."

"But if she thought she were in danger, or if she were angry…"

"No," Rosenkrantz said, shaking his head and frowning. "You met her. She's so small, and gentle, and quiet. Like I said, you hardly ever even know what she's feeling, she just keeps to herself…" The American writer's eyes got soft. "She's practically a kid. She's never run away before…"

Pelleter nodded. "I'll let you know if I find anything."

Rosenkrantz's eyes flashed and his fists closed, his rage returning. "Listen you…" But then he swallowed it back, taking a deep breath. "Thank you," he said.

Pelleter turned to go into the police station, and Rosenkrantz grabbed him by the arm. Pelleter looked back, and this time the American writer just looked sad and scared. He let go of Pelleter's sleeve, and Pelleter went into the station.

A country woman in the waiting area looked up at Pelleter with an imploring, forlorn expression that did not see him.

This was a police station face. It was the same everywhere.

The inspector went behind the counter and into Letreau's office.

"Rosenkrantz was just here," Letreau said, running his hand through his hair, which only caused him to look more harried.

"I saw him outside."

"Now the girl's missing."

Pelleter took a seat.

"I don't like this. Things are happening too fast. There was apparently a reporter around here earlier. One of our local men. The *Vérité* is usually a weekly paper, but they're putting out a special edition about this business. I think my boys know not to talk, but who knows…Do you think we should worry about it?"

"The newspapers don't mean anything."

"The missing girl."

"You can worry if you think it'll make a difference."

"I guess it never does."

"Where's your man from the front desk?"

"Martin? I sent him to Malniveau. Your questions about how much we knew about the prison got me thinking. We need to have somebody on site if this whole thing started there…I told him to demand to see the files, any files, to dig up what he could."

Pelleter nodded his approval, some of his own concern fading from his face. "Good. Very good."

"He left this for you," Letreau said, handing across a paper. "It's not much help, unfortunately."

It was the paper that listed Meranger's known associates. Martin had systematically gone through the entire list, and marked it up to show the present location of all of the people on the list. He had even included a key at the bottom: a cross-out meant the person was dead, a circle meant prison, otherwise he had penciled in their address. Nobody was near Verargent. None of the prisoners were at Malniveau.

"Good," Pelleter said, reading over it. "This is good work."

"It leaves us just where we were before. Knowing nothing."

"Maybe."

"What?"

"Nothing."

There was a knock on the opened door and an officer stood at attention just inside the office.

"What is it?" Letreau said, his frustration spilling over onto the man.

"Sir. Marion is still waiting for you…"

"Oh, I know Marion is waiting for me. Doesn't she know I'm busy here!" He stood, banging his thighs on the underside of his desk. "God damn it!"

He leaned his hands against his thighs, turning his head to the side, a sour expression on his face, biting back the pain.

Pelleter watched his friend. This murder was too much for him.

"And…" the officer started.

"What!"

The young man lowered his voice almost by half, cowed. "We just received a call from a farmer outside of town. It seems that he has found a box in his field."

"So," Letreau said sharply, standing to his full height with a deep intake of breath.

"Well, he said that it seems to him like it may be a coffin. He wants us to come have a look."

Letreau turned to Pelleter, shaking his head. "See, it just keeps getting worse." He turned back to the officer. "Well, go ahead."

"Right, sir," the officer said.

Letreau continued, "I've got to see what Marion wants. She's been waiting all morning."

"Wait." Pelleter stood up, stopping the officer as he turned in the doorway. "Where is this box?"

"On the eastern highway, about ten miles out of town."

Pelleter looked at Letreau. "And about ten miles from the prison." He turned back to the officer. "I think I'll go with you."

By the time Pelleter and the officers arrived at the farm, the farmer and his son had uncovered the whole length of the so-called coffin.

The excavation site was no more than ten feet from the road, halfway between the town and the prison. The officers parked just off of the pavement behind a rusty truck and another automobile already there.

A group of four men and a boy stood around the open grave watching the inspector and the officers approach. The pile of dark brown dirt beside them was like a sixth waiting figure. The mid-afternoon sun had burned away the morning cool, and it was hot in the unshaded field.

"It's a coffin, all right," one of the officers said when they reached the spot. The box was unfinished pine, imperfectly crafted.

"The rain did the first part of the digging for us," the farmer said. He was a mustachioed man of about forty. "My son saw the wood sticking up while he was plowing, and then he came back and got me."

"So you don't know anything about this?" Pelleter said.

"The family plot's back up near the house...This is good soil here. Why would I bury a body where I wanted to plant?"

"And so shallow," one of the other men said.

Pelleter looked at him.

"I'm a neighbor. I was just passing by with my truck. I'll help take it back into town if you need."

Pelleter didn't respond. Instead he looked at the two officers and said, "Open it up."

They looked at him without comprehension, their expressions lost. They had let Pelleter take charge, and did not expect to be called upon.

"Open it," Pelleter said again, throwing up his hands. "We need to know if there's even a body inside, and what it's wearing."

"What it's wearing?" somebody said.

The officers stepped forward, but it was the farmer and his neighbor who each picked up a shovel, and fitted the ends of the blades into the space between the lid of the coffin and its body.

Pelleter stepped away, pacing the ground to the side of the coffin, looking at the dirt as he went.

The sound of wood creaking cut the air, somebody said, "Easy," and then there was a snap.

A car passed on the road heading towards town, slowing as it approached the site where the men's vehicles were parked, and then resuming speed.

"Oh, my god."

Pelleter turned back, and the men parted so he could see.

There was a body in the coffin. It must have been there for several weeks, because the face had softened, distorting the features into a ghost mask, and the body appeared caved in. A large patch of blood stained the man's shirt over his stomach. But the important thing was what the body was wearing: Malniveau Prison grays.

A sweet moldy smell caused more than one man to gag.

Pelleter squatted beside the grave, and pulled the man's shirt taut to reveal the number above the breast. He pulled out his oilcloth notebook and jotted the number down, then he stood and waved a hand towards the body. "Close it back up and get it out of there. This gentleman will take it back to town." And he nodded at the man who had offered his truck.

The officers, embarrassed now over their delay in moving to open the coffin, stepped forward, taking the lid from the farmer. "We've got that. Let the police handle this."

Pelleter began to walk along to the side again, watching the ground. It was clear that he was looking for something by the careful way he stepped, examining each inch of dirt before moving forward.

He called to the boy, who came over at a jog.

"What did you see when you found the box?" he said.

"Just a bit of white, sir. It was the corner sticking up from the ground."

"Look again now. See if you can find anything. You do that side."

The boy ran off to the other side of the grave, and then he also began to pace the ground step by step. The farmer and his neighbors saw what was happening, and they too began to spread out, looking down.

The officers were awkwardly extracting the coffin from its shallow grave.

"Here! Here!"

Everyone looked up. It was one of the men who must have come from the car. He was only a few feet to the west of the grave and several paces closer to the road, looking at Pelleter, waving him over. He knelt.

The whole crowd approached, and the man indicated what he had seen. There was an impossibly straight line in the dirt as though the ground had sunk into a crack. The man was digging with his hand, and he quickly revealed what appeared to be the edge of another coffin.

The group went into action without Pelleter saying anything. The two shovels were brought over, and the farmer and the man who had made the discovery began to dig. Meanwhile, the truck owner helped the officers load the coffin into the bed of his truck, while Pelleter had the boy and the fourth man continue to scan the ground.

The seven-man team fell into a rhythm as will any

group of men who have a large physical task before them, and they worked silently and efficiently, as the sun traversed the sky overhead. Pelleter took his turn with the shovel when it came, but he soon appeared overtaxed, and the men relieved him of the task. He smoked a full cigar, and walked far afield, determined to not leave any of the coffins undiscovered. One was revealed almost twenty feet away.

Cars and trucks passed in both directions on the road, but no one else stopped.

When the fifth box was found, the owner of the truck said, "I hope this is the last of them. My truck can take only one more."

Pelleter had the officers begin to fill in the holes that had been made, while he and the boy went around thrusting the shovel in at random points on the off chance that they would strike wood.

The sun was nearing the horizon, and the weather had once again turned cool. The two men who had come in the car said their goodbyes and left. The officers loaded the last coffin on top of the others in the truck bed.

Pelleter had five numbers written one under the other in his notebook, but one of them he didn't need. He recognized Glamieux at once. As Mahossier had said, his throat had been cut.

"Come on, that's enough," he called.

The boy turned a few feet ahead of him, his spade sticking upright from the earth. The men near where the holes were being filled in looked up as well.

"Fill in the holes, and we're going home. There's no point in working in the dark."

The farmer came up to him nervously. "But what if there are more down there, and we go over them with the plow? You see? I wouldn't want to desecrate the dead."

"You won't."

"But if we uncover one…"

"You let the police know, just like last time. But I think we got them all. We'll know soon enough anyway."

"How?"

"Because we'll be able to ask somebody who knows."

Pelleter walked off before the farmer could ask anything else.

The man with the truck was already on his way back to town.

The graves had been mostly filled in, at least enough to satisfy the farmer whose son would be plowing over them the next day anyway.

"You let us know," Pelleter said again, as he got into the police car. The officer who was driving started the automobile and turned on the lights, which lit the few feet of road just ahead of the car.

Verargent's town square was almost unrecognizable. It was as though it had been an empty stage waiting for its players. A subdued crowd of serious men had gathered around the base of the war monument, spilling into the roadway and blocking traffic. Flickering lights from kerosene lamps and open torches dotted the crowd, casting moving shadows that made the mass of people seem like one large anonymous organism. This was Verargent. With its population spread out over the houses and outlying farms the town could feel abandoned. But brought together, the group was large enough to raise alarm.

The officer driving Pelleter inched the car forward through the throng, forced to let out the clutch again and again. He repeatedly sounded the horn to no effect. The men in the square were unconcerned with allowing the police car through.

The truck carrying the coffins was only just ahead even though it had left the farm a good deal before Pelleter and the young gendarme.

"What is this?" the officer said.

Pelleter caught sight of Letreau huddled with Martin and the mustachioed officer beside the war monument. Letreau had his hands in his overcoat pockets and his shoulders hunched against the brisk April evening.

The car jerked again, the gears groaning.

"Let me out here," Pelleter said, and he released the door. The cool night air rushed into the closed space of the car.

The crackle of the open flames sounded over the murmur of people. Some of the men carried electric torches as well. Pelleter began to push his way towards Letreau.

"Some week to visit Verargent," a man said close at Pelleter's side.

It was Servières. His expression was overjoyed.

"If things keep up like this, we'll have to make the *Vérité* a daily."

"You would like that."

They were almost to Letreau now, but Letreau and his men were breaking apart.

Pelleter would not ask the reporter what had happened. He would know soon enough.

"Have you seen this evening's edition?" Servières said, and then a copy was floating in front of Pelleter. The headline, which took up almost all of the space above the fold read:

## ESCAPED CONVICT MURDERED
## IN THE STREET

Pelleter did not reach for the paper, but Servières forced it on him. "Please. Please take it."

Pelleter folded the paper and stuffed it into his coat pocket. They were through the crowd to where Letreau had been standing, but Letreau was now atop the bottom step of the monument's base calling over the crowd.

"Gentlemen! Gentlemen!"

The mass of noise dropped, but it was tentative, the crowd unsure if they had been called to order.

"Gentlemen!"

The silence spread then in a ripple from the spot where Letreau was standing, out to the back of the group where the square started once again. All eyes turned to the chief of police.

"I want to thank all of you for coming out like this."

There was a renewed murmur, and Letreau held up his hand.

"I know we would each want the same if it was our children."

Children? So this did not have to do with Meranger?

"As you have all heard, Marion Perreaux's two little boys Georges and Albert have gone missing. They were last seen Tuesday afternoon at Monsieur Marque's sweet shop here in town, and they were to walk back to the Perreaux farm in time for supper."

Letreau spoke with calm and command, so different than in his office earlier. Organizing a search party was in his purview, a murder investigation was beyond him.

"Everyone should split into three-man teams and search from here outward. If you locate the boys and can bring them back here, do so at once. If they are injured, two men stay with the boys and the third man should come here to get help. Everyone should return to report at sunrise regardless of what they have found. Are there any questions?"

There was a moment's pause in which a murmur began.

"Okay, let's get to it."

The crowd began to split, talking and shouting in an indecipherable cacophony.

Pelleter pushed his way to where Letreau was stepping down from the monument by leaning on the shoulder of one of his men. Servières stayed close to Pelleter's side, but Pelleter paid him no attention.

When he finally reached Letreau, Pelleter said, "Our case just got a lot more complicated." He did not want to mention the details of the five bodies in front of Servières, although it was unlikely that the man had not seen the loaded-down truck make its way through the square towards the hospital.

"I can't be concerned with that now," Letreau said. "Meranger is dead. Those boys might still be alive. You can search or meet up with me in the morning."

Pelleter nodded once. Letreau was right that if the boys were alive, that was the priority.

"I'll search."

Letreau nodded, but he had already turned back to his junior officers.

The square had emptied out and taken on its normal sleepy quiet. The only thing out of place was the occasional raised voice a block or two away that indicated that the town was not at rest.

"I'll search with you," Servières said.

Pelleter looked at him, and then started away. "Fine."

"What about our third?"

Pelleter turned back. "You," he called to Officer Martin.

Martin looked around him to see if Pelleter had meant someone else. Then he jogged over to Pelleter. "Sir?"

"Have you been assigned a duty?"

"No, sir."

"You're with us. Lead the way to Benoît's house. I want to see where you found Meranger's body."

# 6.

## *Hansel and Gretel*

The three men walked in silence down the center of the street. Martin led the way, a half a pace out in front, and Pelleter and Servières hurried side by side. The chief inspector walked with his head down, an unlit half-smoked cigar clenched in his teeth, his jaw moving in contemplation. Servières watched him.

The air was heavy with moisture, and a slight breeze was enough for a chill to cut through the men's clothes.

The occasional call, "Georges! Albert!", echoed in the streets.

"Should we be looking?" Servières said.

They had passed two other search parties on their route, each deliberately examining the alleys towards the center of town.

Pelleter said, "If those boys are to be found, they're not going to be found in plain sight a few blocks from the square."

Servières did not reply.

They were in a completely residential area now, a quiet street at the edge of town lined with two-story homes built much closer together than necessary. There were no streetlamps. The few lit windows in the surrounding homes did little to light the street.

Martin stopped, looking at the ground. He then looked

at the house which they were standing in front of. "This is the spot," he said.

It was exactly as it had been described to Pelleter, complete with the details he had filled in himself, such as the broken trellis beside the baker's front door. If there had been anything to see, it would have long since been washed away by the rain. He could just see the tracks of mud on the baker's driveway, where the water had streamed from the street into the house.

"Spread out. Look around," Pelleter said.

Martin started for the opposite side of the street.

"What are we looking for?" Servières said.

"The children."

Even in this residential district, it was as Pelleter had said. There were no places where the children could be hidden for long. The spaces between the homes were little more than alleys, and the houses on the neighboring streets backed up almost to the rear stoop of the houses in Benoît's street.

Pelleter took special care to examine any external basement entrances, but most were locked.

Servières began to call "Georges! Albert!" and soon Martin took up the call as well. No one would get much sleep in Verargent tonight.

Pelleter was three houses down from the baker's now, using the back alley for passage. He found an unlocked basement, and looked up at the house. There were no lights on. He knocked on the back door, and then, satisfied, he pulled open the basement, folding the hatch back onto the ground.

"Hello!" he called. The basement was pitch black. The

dank smell of wet earth and mildew rose to meet him. There were no children's voices.

He took a few steps down, and ducked his head to enter the small space, the earthen floor soft beneath his shoes.

As his eyes adjusted, he could see why the door had been left unlocked. There seemed to be nothing in the shadows. He lit a match to be sure, and used it to light his cigar. Nothing. Not even a coal box or a modest wine rack.

He shook out the match, and stood for a moment in the dark, enjoying the warmth of the cigar. If nothing else, it was as if he had seen Benoît's basement. But there was nothing to be learned here. He needed to get a medical examiner to come and work on those bodies. He needed to talk with the prisoner who had been stabbed that morning. He needed to find out how Meranger got out of Malniveau. Only if he went back to his hotel to get the sleep he needed for the next day, then Servières would be all too happy to report in the *Vérité*, Inspector Pelleter uninterested in saving lost boys.

He forced his mind to pass over his instinct to link the missing children to the dead bodies.

There were too many people missing—the warden, Madame Rosenkrantz... Who else?

Pelleter made his way back to the gutter where Meranger had been found. Away from Servières, he squatted to see if he could find anything that had been missed, even in this low light. He paced the edge of the street, still squatting, but there was nothing out of the ordinary grit and grime.

Martin returned. "No sign of them, sir."

Pelleter did not answer.

"Did you find something?"

Pelleter stood to his full height, stretching his back. "I didn't expect to. But I still wanted to see."

"It was raining really hard," Martin said. "The water pooled around him, about here." He pointed. The young officer wanted to know that he had not missed something crucial, that he had not made a mistake.

"It's okay," Pelleter said. "There's nothing here."

Servières called from halfway down the block, hurrying towards them, "What are we doing now?" He did not want to miss anything.

"We keep moving," and this time Pelleter led the way, away from the town center, passing Servières before he had a chance to turn around.

The Benoîts were really at the edge of town. Only a few houses away from the baker's, the paved road gave way to a dirt road cut through fields. There was enough light from the stars to see by.

"Were we even looking for the Perreaux children or are you still continuing your murder investigation?" Servières said.

"You take that side of the road," Pelleter said to Martin, ignoring Servières. "Keep your eye on the ground and ahead, but don't leave the road."

"Because it seemed to me like you were awfully interested in that patch of ground, and it was clear that there weren't any children there."

Pelleter turned to Servières, "You take that side."

Distracted by the command, Servières dropped to the side of the road, scanning the darkened field beside him.

"What are we doing?" Servières said in a loud voice. To have any kind of conversation spread out along the road as they were required them to raise their voices.

"Searching."

The fields here were of wild grass as high as a man in places. Off in the distance, black blotches were islands of trees rooted in the otherwise open expanse. Leaving the road at night would be foolish, but if the boys had not been located by the morning, those small patches of woods would have to be searched. If Georges and Albert had gotten that far away from town, they would have likely stopped at the edge of the woods for shelter.

"Georges!" Martin cried. "Albert!" The sudden noise left the night silent.

"When those boys are found, they're going to have a lot of people angry at them," Servières said.

"If…" Pelleter started.

"If what," Servières said, looking at the chief inspector.

Pelleter said nothing. The end of his cigar burned a bright orange and then faded.

"Oh." Servières had put it together. "Georges and Albert went missing on Tuesday night—" Servières took out his notebook and held it close to his face to take notes.

"That's the same night Meranger was found," Martin said, excited now that he had caught on too.

"So we *were* looking for the children," Servières said as he wrote. "Because if they had seen something, like who dumped Meranger's body…"

"Keep your eyes on the side of the road," Pelleter ordered.

Servières brought down the pad in surprise, then put

it away without comment. He really was not a bad sort. He was just a man who loved his job.

There was a tense silence for a moment, and then it passed into the silence of a shared task. A cry of "Albert!" came from the distance behind them. The moon was high in the sky. It must have been near to midnight.

"It poured that night," Martin said, almost to himself. Then he called, "Georges! Albert! Georges! Albert! Your mother is worried for you! Call if you hear me! It's Officer Martin!"

There was nothing.

The damp had gotten into their clothing, and Pelleter hunched his shoulders against the cold.

"You probably think this is a bit below you," Servières said. "In the city, you have a whole team of men to do this kind of thing for you. Didn't I just read you solved a case because your wife had found the suspects?"

Pelleter said nothing.

"A double homicide solved by your wife."

"It's still the chief inspector who organizes the investigation and must take the responsibility," Martin said, rising to Pelleter's defense.

"I asked the chief inspector about responsibility last night, and he got very angry with me."

"Reporters!" Martin said, as though he had been troubled by reporters his whole career.

"What were you doing in Verargent before Meranger had even been murdered?" Servières asked Pelleter suddenly in the hard tone he had used in the café before. "There's something happening here, and you knew something before anyone else."

"Perhaps it was a coincidence," Pelleter said.

"It was not a coincidence. You went out to the prison to see Mahossier. I know that. I also know about the other two times you came to see him, and the two cases that were solved, the bank robbery and the woman murderer. You see I'm not as provincial as you thought. I know some things."

Martin was watching the two men as they walked. No one was searching the side of the road anymore.

"What did Mahossier tell you?"

Pelleter did not like to be questioned, least of all by a reporter. It was his job to interrogate people, not to be interrogated.

"Tell me. I'll find out anyway."

Pelleter stopped and pivoted towards Servières. "Watch the side of the road!" He then raised his chin and cried, "Georges! Albert!" and continued on.

The two other men fell into place to either side of him, once again scanning the flowing gray grass.

"Did…" Martin started, but then shook his head.

Servières was still smarting. "You have no call to yell at me," he said. "I apologized about last night."

"What happened last night?" Martin said, forgetting himself.

"I posed as a hotel guest and I asked the inspector some questions about Mahossier. About what it was like."

Martin did not respond, perhaps embarrassed that he had also asked Pelleter about the case the day before, but his own curiosity was apparent in his silence.

"This was big news here," Servières said. "I know it was big news everywhere, we followed the case like all the other papers, but when it became clear that Mahossier might end up in Malniveau…We followed it long after everyone else had dropped it…People were angry. They know it's a federal prison over there. They know that there are bad men who have done bad things. But they don't stop to think about it. It's vague. What this man had done could not be ignored."

"But they ignore it now."

"Except when you show up."

"And why would anybody know when and why I showed up?"

"The people have a right to know."

"Are you going to hide behind that again?"

Servières did not respond. His face was turned away, scanning the side of the road for any sign of the missing children.

Pelleter softened his voice, and tried a different tack. "Do you pay attention to what's going on out at the prison then? My understanding was that there wasn't much intercourse between the town and prison."

"We don't report on every little incident out there if that's what you mean. Half of the *Vérité* is devoted to the school's football scores and the church's bake sale."

"And the train station," Martin said.

"There's never going to be a train station."

"The town officials love it when you point that out."

Pelleter blew a plume of smoke, thick in the night air. "So Fournier…"

"The assistant warden?" Servières said, trying to read Pelleter's expression. "What about him?"

Pelleter made a theatrical shrug. "What about him?"

"He keeps to himself. He practically lives at the prison. We did a profile on him when he first moved here, but it was a dry c.v. He took his degree here. He worked at this shipping firm. He worked at this prison. There was nothing interesting about the man, and he has not made any attempt to get to know any of the people here since. He seems like a particular administrator and nothing more."

Pelleter nodded, but only because Servières' description fit his own idea of the man. If anything, it was more banal, not taking into account how violent Fournier's particularity was. But a violent passion was different than a violent man, and sometimes the reverse, as Pelleter knew all too well. Still, he did not like that the assistant warden had kept him from interviewing the stabbed prisoner or that he was in control of what information was at hand. He turned to Martin. "What do you think?"

Martin stood up straighter, wanting to please and forgetting to scan his section of the road. "The Assistant Warden? He seems very good at his job. He knows everything that's supposed to be done, and what's actually getting done."

Except he did not know that five of his prisoners were dead and buried in a field. Or maybe he had known and had not felt that it was necessary to mention.

"He always acts angry about it, but he lets me see everything I ask for."

The tip of Pelleter's cigar glowed orange again. It was close enough to his face now to cast an eerie light on his features. They were tense in contemplation.

"This is pointless," Servières said, throwing up his hands.

An engine sounded in the distance behind them. Martin and Servières both looked back to see headlights as a single distant speck, and the dots of light that marked the town floating in the silhouette against the blue night sky.

Pelleter inhaled deeply on his cigar, pulling the flame into the last of the tobacco. He then dropped the butt in a puddle standing in one of the ruts of the uneven road.

"What about Rosenkrantz? Is he big news, one of the other local celebrities along with Mahossier?"

Servières turned back. The sound of the engine grew steadily, but it was still a good distance off.

"People don't care much about an American, or a writer. His books aren't translated into French either. His wife is something to look at, though. And there was some scandal there. They married when she was barely eighteen, a girl. He left his wife for her too. But she's learned to carry herself like a much older woman."

"So you wouldn't think that he would kill his father-in-law?"

"No, I wouldn't think it. But what does that mean?"

"Nothing."

"Exactly."

Pelleter was beginning to like Servières a little. His stunt the night before was just the kind of thing Pelleter would have tried if it served his purpose.

"I understand why you have to look at Rosenkrantz, but I wouldn't expect too much of him. He makes Fournier look like a society man, except when he's on his rare drinking sprees, but then they usually go to the city for that."

"When was the last time that happened?"

"Four, maybe five months ago."

The engine was loud enough now that Pelleter looked back to see how close it was. He started to get over to the side by Martin.

"Won't you give me one quote," Servières begged, "about Mahossier? People out here were indignant, but they really can't imagine what it must have been like to find those cages and the pit."

"And the boy still alive," Pelleter said.

"Yes. And that." But Servières seemed unable to actually say boy or child.

"When Mahossier was brought here, my mother wouldn't let me out of the house for a week," Martin said beside Pelleter. "And I was thirteen!"

The headlights resolved and it was a truck that was almost on them.

"Wait a second," Martin said.

Servières at the last moment decided to jump and join them on their side of the road, a shadow dancing across the headlights.

"Do you think Mahossier…" Martin said, upset.

"There *are* two boys missing," Servières said.

"We should go back," Martin said. "Perhaps Chief Letreau didn't think to check the prison."

The truck pulled to a stop beside them, and the man in the driver's seat rolled down his window. There were two other men beside him, although their faces could not be seen.

"You find anything out this way?"

"No, Jean," Martin started, "but—"

Pelleter gripped Martin's shoulder, cutting the young man off. He glanced at Servières, but there was no need to worry there. Servières understood how information could be used to stir up the public and the value of releasing that information at just the right moment.

"They haven't found anything back in town either. I offered to drive out a good ways to extend the search, and some other people were going to drive out on the highway too."

"We'll cover the next few hundred yards," Pelleter said. "You go on."

"We're not going to find anything at night anyway," one of the other men said from the darkness of the truck.

"Madame Perreaux is hysterical," Jean said. "I heard they gave her something to calm her down, but Letreau promised that we would search all night if we had to."

Martin said, "Thanks, Jean," as though he had the power to thank the men on behalf of the Verargent gendarmes.

Jean nodded, and began to roll up his window, bobbing in his seat with the activity even as he released the clutch and let the truck begin to roll forward.

When the taillights were a good deal ahead of them, Pelleter said, "I saw Mahossier at the prison myself this morning. He's not involved in this."

"But two boys missing and just when we found that a prisoner had gotten out of Malniveau—"

"That's not what this is," Pelleter barked.

Martin closed his mouth, and looked away.

It was hard to tell in the light from the moon, but Servières looked pale.

"That's not what this is," Pelleter said again. But he had been thinking the same thing from the moment he heard the boys were missing. For two young boys to go missing with Mahossier close by...

Pelleter took control again. "Let's finish this. I'll take that side this time, Monsieur Servières. You join young Martin here. We don't have far to go."

He pointed. The red taillights of the truck were small, but still visible in the distance. They had only to cover the ground that would not be covered by the men in the truck.

They spread out and began to pace along slowly without speaking. The distant sound of voices would sometimes reach them when the wind blew, but the words were indecipherable. The movement of the grass was like the sound of a poorly tuned wireless.

The more they looked, the more Pelleter felt like the man in the truck, that they would find nothing at night.

Across the road, Martin and Servières began to talk in quiet tones that did not reach the chief inspector. He may have heard the name Mahossier, or it might have still been weighing on his mind.

Georges and Albert Perreaux. They had never determined the name of the boy they had found in the cage in Mahossier's basement.

A sudden gust of wind cut them hard, the grass yelling in anger. The tension in Pelleter's neck and shoulders from the cold pained him. It was time to turn back.

They continued forward.

Servières laughed, and Martin then joined him.

Pelleter shivered. If Mahossier was involved, the boys

wouldn't be out here somewhere, they would be in town in a basement. He had searched the one basement, but all of the others had been locked. They would have to be opened.

Pelleter thought of the cages...small prisons...

"Servières," Pelleter called.

It silenced the two men's laughter, and they stopped to face the chief inspector.

"You want a quote about Mahossier?"

Servières' face turned somber then. He slapped his chest to feel for his pad.

The chief inspector spoke before he had found it.

"It was a horror."

# 7.

## *Visiting Hours*

The morning found Verargent soaked in sunlight, but Pelleter could tell even from his hotel room that there was a nip still in the air by the way the people in the square walked with their hands in their pockets and their elbows pulled tight to their bodies.

Pelleter left the hotel still pulling on his overcoat, a troubled expression across his brow. He shoved his hands in his pockets against the chill, and found a wad of folded paper there. He pulled it out. It was the newspaper Servières had pushed on him the night before.

### ESCAPED CONVICT MURDERED
### IN THE STREET

After last night's unsuccessful manhunt, this seemed like old news. But it was big news for a town like Verargent, and the *Vérité* had treated it accordingly, devoting the entire front page and most of page two and three to the article. The byline was Philippe Servières.

It was all speculation, although none of the facts were incorrect. They had interviewed the baker. They had Meranger's name and history. They mentioned the Rosenkrantzes by name, although they didn't yet have Clotilde's disappearance. Pelleter figured the paper could expect to hear from an irate Monsieur Rosenkrantz today anyway. Otherwise there was nothing new.

There were also public opinions, and a brief history that recounted the three previous escape attempts from Malniveau much as they had been described to Pelleter the first day of the investigation.

Pelleter refolded the paper and stuffed it back into his pocket. He didn't see how it would affect his investigation one way or the other, but he still didn't like it. Newspapermen were just sensationalist leeches.

There was a tired group of men standing outside of police headquarters, smoking cigarettes in silence. This was what was left of the volunteer search party, men who could put off their day's work or had no work to go to.

Pelleter went inside. The entire Verargent police department was there behind the desk that divided the public space from the department offices. Officer Martin tried to catch Pelleter's eye, but Pelleter ignored him, intent on Letreau's office.

Letreau was squatting before a tearful woman who Pelleter recognized as the woman that had been waiting the day before as he left to investigate the coffins in the field. Madame Perreaux, no doubt. Had that been just yesterday? There was too much happening too fast without enough answers.

Pelleter lit a cigar, and leaned in a corner beside a filing cabinet without a word.

"We will find them no matter what," Letreau was saying, as the woman shook her head back and forth, back and forth. "We will find them, but you need to let me give my men orders."

Madame Perreaux shook her head again. She was hysterical.

Letreau came to the same conclusion, and stood with the woman still shaking her head, tears pouring down her face. He looked over at Pelleter with grave eyes, and then took a step towards the door.

Pelleter met him in the doorway, and put a hand on his friend's shoulder.

"You must search the basements."

"What basements?"

"All of the basements."

"I was going to do another concentric circle search based from the Perreaux farm. If that was where they were heading from the sweet shop and they got lost, it's most likely they're out there."

Pelleter nodded. He could not argue with that. As he had told Martin and Servières the night before, Mahossier was in prison; he most likely had nothing to do with this. Still, the basements needed to be checked.

"Then assign only two or three officers to check the basements. Whatever you can spare."

"What are you thinking?"

Pelleter looked back at Madame Perreaux, who was still bawling, twisting a handkerchief in her lap. He pulled Letreau out of the office.

"If they got lost, you're right, they're probably somewhere close to home. But if they got taken…"

"You think this is a kidnapping?"

"I think we need to search everywhere."

"Fine. You can have four men. I'm going to organize the rest."

Pelleter shook his head. "I'm going to Malniveau."

Letreau lost his cool then, puffing out his cheeks. "Pelleter, I have six dead prisoners in my jurisdiction and two missing children! I've said it before, I appreciate your help, but I'm not sure I see how you're helping."

Pelleter ignored this outburst. "I'll take a taxi to the prison. Search the basements."

Letreau's cheeks puffed out again, and his eyes blazed.

Pelleter said nothing. Letreau had a tendency to get overwhelmed, but in the end he was a good policeman. He would do what Pelleter had suggested, because he knew that Pelleter might be right.

The chief inspector pushed his way back through the officers towards the front door. As he did, he heard Letreau begin to give orders behind him.

Verargent's sole taxi sat parked outside the café across the square. As Pelleter reached for the rear door handle, the driver came out of the café straightening his paper-boy hat.

"Malniveau Prison."

Pelleter settled in to the backseat relieved that the driver was one of the astute drivers rarely found in provincial towns, who knew when his fare preferred silence to small talk.

He pulled out his oilskin notebook, and added the details he had been too tired to add the night before.

His notes ended:

*Thursday morning another prisoner is knifed at the prison…Nobody can agree on the number of prisoners stabbed or killed in the last month.*

He corrected himself so that the entry read, *Thursday, April 6, approx. 10 AM*. It wouldn't do to be imprecise. With so many happenings, it would be important to know exactly when everything took place. He continued:

> *Approx. 1 PM — Coffin uncovered in field halfway between Malniveau Prison and Verargent. Further investigation reveals a total of five coffins containing murdered prisoners.*

The chief inspector looked out the window at the passing landscape. It was so uniform that it was incredible to him that whoever had buried the bodies had been able to locate the same burial ground each time, since he was convinced that the bodies had been buried on five separate occasions. He would know for sure when the medical examiner had examined the corpses.

> *Tuesday, April 4, Approx 5 PM — Georges Perreaux (six years old) and Albert Perreaux (five years old) go missing. Last seen at Monsieur Marque's sweet shop.*

Letreau had interviewed Monsieur Marque himself. He assured Pelleter that Monsieur Marque was in no way involved with the children's disappearance. And why would he be? In a small town like Verargent the owner of the candy store could not afford to have a bad reputation with regards to children.

Pelleter turned back to his earlier entries, and tried to fit in the margin beside the entry on Madame Rosenkrantz's visit to the hotel,

> *Last time Madame Rosenkrantz is seen.*

He did the same for the warden beside the entry on Mahossier's claim that prisoners were being systematically murdered.

He looked at what he had written, and he felt the anger well up in him again. It was time to take the offensive. There was too much going on, and up until now they had been reacting. Events happened and they tried to keep up. Even the manhunt the night before was a reaction. But today, at least, he would find out what Mahossier knew.

To calm himself he started at the beginning and reviewed everything so far, but it didn't help. He knew what had happened in many instances, but he did not know why or how, and therefore he did not know who. He knew nothing.

The prison loomed before them. The taxi drove up to the gate, and Pelleter got out, instructing the driver to return in two hours and to wait if he was not yet ready. The chief inspector showed his documents to the guard at the outer gate, crossed the space where several cars were parked, moss and wild grass growing in places from between the cobbles, and then he showed his documents again at the inner door, where he was admitted to the prison.

"I hear there was more excitement in town last night," Remy said.

"Any excitement out here?"

"Oh, it's always exciting here."

"That's what I thought."

Pelleter passed in to the administrative offices. The young woman at the first desk took one look at him and reached for the phone. She was a plain girl who would have been prettier if she had had the conviction to either cut her hair shorter or to grow it longer. Instead she had settled on an awkward style that paid homage to a bob without being one.

She whispered into the receiver with her head bowed, blocking her mouth with the closed fist of her free hand.

There was a kind of lethargy in the rest of the office that came perhaps from some of the men having been involved in the search the night before, but Pelleter had spent enough time in police stations, courts, and prisons to know that the usual situation in those places was of utter boredom.

He saw a desk towards the back of the room stacked with files. This, no doubt, was Officer Martin's workspace. The prison workers had been unsure if they were allowed to clean it up yet. Pelleter made a mental note to get Officer Martin back out here as soon as possible. Even if he found nothing, it was better to have someone on hand.

The young woman replaced the receiver of the phone, and sat up rod straight as though the phone cradle were a switch attached to her spine. She looked up at the chief inspector with pursed lips, took a breath, and said, "Monsieur Fournier is otherwise engaged at the moment, and does not know when he will be available to assist you. He suggests that you come back another time."

She waited then, as if to see if she had passed some recitation exam.

Pelleter could not help but smile, and the girl slumped a little sensing that she had failed.

"That's fine," the chief inspector said. "I wasn't here to see Monsieur Fournier anyway. I can just show myself around," and he began to turn back to the door.

"But…"

"No need to bother," Pelleter continued in his light tone. He pointed at the door. "I'm on my way to the infirmary. I know the way."

The young woman looked around at her colleagues, imploring for help. They were paying attention now, but only with surreptitious glances that relieved them of any responsibility.

As Pelleter pushed open the office door, the young woman stood up behind her desk but did not move. He turned back. "You could do me one favor," he said as though it were an afterthought. "I'll need to see Mahossier again. Please have him brought down."

The woman's shoulders sank, but Pelleter did not wait for an answer. As he stepped back into the entry hall, he could only just see one of the other men stand behind her.

"Open this door for me, Remy. I'm going to the infirmary." Pelleter tried to remember if there was another locked door between this one and the infirmary, but he thought it best to keep moving and worry about it when the time came. If the young woman had recovered herself, she no doubt was on the phone to Fournier once again, and it was only a matter of a few minutes before the assistant warden made an appearance.

As Remy unlocked the inner door, Pelleter said, "Could you be sure that they're bringing Mahossier down to the interrogation room for me as well. There seemed to be some confusion about that in the office."

"I'm sure there was," Remy said, smiling. "There needs to be a paper for everything, and god forbid if you miss one little paper." Remy pulled open the door, stepping aside to allow the chief inspector to pass.

Just as he was about to step into the hall, the office door jerked open and one of the clerks appeared. He pulled himself up short in an attempt to regain some composure, and then he said, "Right this way, Monsieur Pelleter."

They must have decided that it was safest to have somebody accompany the chief inspector if he was going to force his way into the prison. Or perhaps Fournier had given the order that Pelleter was to be watched. In either case, the young man stepped ahead of Pelleter, and then led the way to the left towards the infirmary.

"Any more incidents since yesterday?" Pelleter asked the nervous young man from one step behind him.

The man did not turn. "Incidents, sir?"

"What's your name?"

"Monsieur Vittier."

"Okay, Vittier. Fights, stabbings, murders. Incidents."

"I'm sure I can't say, sir."

"I'm sure you can't."

They came to a steel partition with a door in it that divided the hall into equal intervals. Vittier fumbled with a ring of keys he produced from his pocket. So there *had* been another locked doorway before coming to the infirmary. Then Pelleter was glad for the chaperone.

Vittier managed to get the door open, and this time Pelleter stepped through first. The air in this stretch of the hallway had a bottled-up mustiness to it, cut with the ammoniac smell coming from the infirmary.

Pelleter strode along the hall, unconcerned as to whether Vittier was with him. The door to the infirmary stood open. Apparently it was assumed injured prisoners were in too much pain to try to escape.

In the infirmary, there was none of the hurried excitement from the day before. A guard sat in a straight-backed chair just inside the doorway. The stabbing victim was the only prisoner taking up one of the four cots. He was small, pale, and gaunt, as though he had been in hospital for weeks instead of twenty-four hours.

Pelleter crossed the room and set himself on the edge of the cot beside the prisoner. He saw that the prisoner was handcuffed to the bed.

Vittier came up beside him, standing at the foot of the bed.

Pelleter held out his papers, but the prisoner, whose eyes darted between Pelleter and Vittier, showed no inclination towards reading what was held before him.

"I am Chief Inspector Pelleter with the Central Bureau. I've come from the city to look into things here. I was hoping you could tell me something of what happened yesterday."

The prisoner's eyes again darted between Pelleter and Vittier. No other part of him moved. His face remained blank. He seemed unimpressed with Pelleter's credentials.

"Do you know who it was who stabbed you?"

The man turned his head away from the chief inspector, wincing as he did.

Pelleter shifted his weight on the cot. The metal rod of the frame cut into the back of his thighs.

"Vittier!"

The young man jerked towards Pelleter. He had been lost in contemplation of the prisoner's wasted form. Now he looked as though he were awaiting a sentence of his own. Was it the prison itself that made everyone here somber, or did Fournier have his men—both his staff and his prisoners—on edge at all times?

"Give us a moment," Pelleter said, and he nodded his head in the direction of the door.

The young clerk went to the entrance and stood beside the guard. They did not speak to one another.

Pelleter leaned forward then, his elbows on his knees, and lowered his voice. "Can you tell me who stabbed you?"

For a moment it seemed as though the prisoner was going to act as though he had not heard the repeated question. But at last, without turning his head, he said just above a whisper, "I don't know."

"Do you know why you were stabbed?"

The prisoner closed his eyes and shook his head. He had been thinking about it, and he didn't know. Prison gave a man lots of time to think, but almost getting killed must make him think in new ways.

"What about the other men that were killed? Are people saying anything about them?"

There was another long pause, and Pelleter was worried that he would have to start from the beginning again. But at last the wounded man said, "No one's saying anything."

"If you say something," Pelleter said, leaning even further forward until he felt the cot begin to tip beneath him, "then maybe I can help."

Still there was no reaction.

"No one will know it was you. I'm going to talk to other prisoners as well."

The man turned his head quickly towards Pelleter now, his eyes wide. "I don't know anything. It was crowded in the yard. It could have been anyone who went for me. I had no beef. I don't know nothing else."

"Okay," Pelleter said.

The whites of the man's eyes showed around large pupils, his nostrils flared, the look of a man afraid and in pain and backed into a corner.

"Okay." The chief inspector stood. He watched the man carefully. "But this will probably be the last chance I have to talk to you without Assistant Warden Fournier."

There was no reaction. The man's face remained the same, full of pain and indignation. Fournier's name had changed nothing.

The chief inspector considered the man for another moment, frustrated that he had not learned anything more from him. With each new incident, Pelleter seemed to know less, and even the victims were ignorant. Sometimes there was nothing that could be done on a case—it was just a matter of waiting—but Pelleter was unwilling to believe that was true here. Too many things were happening, and somebody knew why. It was just a matter of asking the right person the questions in the right way.

Pelleter turned away from the man on the cot.

"Vittier," he called. "Take me to Mahossier."

Mahossier was already in the examination room, his hands and legs once again chained. To Pelleter's surprise, Monsieur le Directeur Adjoint Fournier had still not made an appearance. Pelleter left Vittier with the guard outside the door, and took up a position behind Mahossier and just to the side.

"Why did you stab the man in the yard?" Pelleter said.

Mahossier made no attempt to turn around. "Why, Inspector! I'm surprised at you. Surely you know that I didn't have yard privileges yesterday. Some days I do, some days I don't. Monsieur Fournier sees to that. It's for my own protection, you see. Some of the boys here don't like me very much. I couldn't say why."

Pelleter could hear the hilarity in Mahossier's voice. The criminal did not seem put out to have Pelleter behind him. Pelleter was in no mood to be toyed with. He tried to keep his voice calm. "What do you do those days for meals? Are you allowed in the mess?"

"One of the good boys brings it to me in my cell, but assistant warden's careful for it to be a different one as often as possible. What's the matter? He didn't tell you any of this? Is he not being helpful?"

Pelleter would not be drawn in.

Mahossier put on a tone of absolute concern. "Have

they found those two little boys yet? I've been so worried about them."

"And how do you know about the missing children?"

"How is Madame Pelleter by the way? Well, I trust. But why wouldn't she be?"

Pelleter grabbed Mahossier by the shoulders then, and threw him to the side, causing the prisoner to fall heavily to the floor, his head knocking the stone with a dull thump, followed a second after by the clatter of the chair falling to the ground. With his hands chained to his legs, Mahossier was forced to remain in a fetal position in the shadow of the table, a small old man, unable to even raise himself.

Pelleter kicked the chair, which had settled partially on Mahossier, into the corner.

The old man was shaking, laughing soundlessly.

Pelleter circled the table to prevent himself from kicking the downed man. He thought of Servières asking him that first night how he could be in the same room with this monster and not kill him. The thought cooled his anger. The play had been made, and it was not a bad one. He would see what effect it had.

He came around so that he was standing in front of Mahossier's face. The murderer, still laughing, was straining to see the floor beneath his head.

"Very good," he said. "I think I'm bleeding." He licked the cold stone, and his grin spread even wider. "I am bleeding! Very good." And he laughed some more.

Pelleter squatted before Mahossier and said the one thing he thought might force a straight answer out of the man. "I will leave on tonight's train. I don't have to be a part of any of this."

"I suppose you could," Mahossier said from his place on the floor. "Whether you have to be a part of it...that depends on what the press thinks and what the Central Bureau thinks about what the press thinks when Le Maire and Letreau and Le Directeur decide that it would be nice if it was the fault of that detective from the city that several dead bodies turned up and several people went missing. It's true you have no obligation to me."

Mahossier thought he had Pelleter in his control and the chief inspector bristled at the notion.

"But you know these small towns...It never seems to be the people in charge, just people drifting through."

"Now you're a political activist? Or is it a social re-former?"

"I prefer concerned citizen." The shadows on his cheek deepened as a grin spread. "I love the word concerned. It's so...useful."

Pelleter stood to relieve the ache that had begun to burn in his thighs from squatting. He pulled out the still-standing chair, the one that he had sat in two days prior, and sat down. From there he could not see Mahossier, but instead, looked across the table at the sweating stone wall across from him. The rough-hewn faces of the stones were a miniature topography in which an ant could be lost forever. From his point of view, able to take in the whole wall's surface, Pelleter did not think it made any more sense to him than it would to the ant.

Mahossier filled the silence. His one weakness when

he felt as though he had a worthy conversationalist. "I don't know anything about those missing boys. They have nothing to do with this."

"Then if you know about everything else, wouldn't it be easier to tell me?"

"I don't know about everything else."

"Then what do you know about?"

"Dead prisoners."

"I know about them too."

"See, you're not a total loss, Chief Inspector. And I was trying to come to terms with the disappointment."

It was easier to talk to the man without being able to see him, his voice floating up from below.

"Who moved the bodies?" Mahossier said.

That was the question. But he responded, "Who killed the men?"

"Perhaps..." Delight returned to Mahossier's voice again, as though ice cream had been suggested and the question was now which flavor. "Perhaps you answer my question and I'll answer yours!"

"You're not worried about being a snitch?"

Mahossier's delight turned to anger. "Listen, detective! I am already reviled. I told you that to start. But being reviled isn't always a bad thing."

Pelleter wondered how that could be. Still, Mahossier had highlighted once again the question that seemed most pressing. How had those prisoners' bodies gotten out of Malniveau? Who had moved them?

Pelleter contemplated the wall. After a few moments, Mahossier began to hum, and the tune eventually penetrated the chief inspector's thoughts. It was a children's tune. If Pelleter remembered correctly it was about going to grandmother's house.

Pelleter stood, his chair scraping the floor, cutting off Mahossier's song.

He had learned nothing here. The initial summons, the oblique aspersions regarding the assistant warden…it all seemed to be for Mahossier's own amusement, and Pelleter was jumping through his hoops like an amateur.

The chief inspector went to the door. He raised his hand to knock, but held it there, suspended in the air. A noise came from the other side of the table, a shuffle, and the clank of chain on stone, but Pelleter could not see what Mahossier was doing.

"Mahossier," Pelleter barked.

The movement stopped.

"If those boys don't turn up soon, and alive, you may find that you have yard privileges every day again."

There was no response from the floor.

"Or perhaps the next time I send guards in here to pick you up off the floor, I'll only have to follow your body to find out how they get dead prisoners out of Malniveau."

With that, Pelleter allowed his fist to drop against the metal door, a hollow echoing clang, signaling that he was ready to go.

# 8.

## Lost and Found

The temperature had climbed so that the brow of Pelleter's hat was clammy and a faint sheen of sweat coated his body beneath his overcoat as he stepped out of the taxi in front of the café. It was the humidity that was particularly oppressive. Most of the sky was clear, but to the east there was a dirty-sheep-colored expanse of clouds that may or may not have threatened rain.

Verargent Square was quiet, the town about its post-lunch business. Only the old men who lined the base of the monument were to be seen, and they were as still as the statue above them.

The café was equally silent. Pelleter ordered some beer and a ham and cheese sandwich for carry away. He wanted to get back to the police station to find out any news about the missing children. He also needed to send Martin back to the prison files and to call Lambert at the Central Bureau.

The waitress appeared from the back and the proprietor bullied her to fetch the inspector's meal.

Pelleter pulled out his watch. One o'clock, three days after the first body was found. This was the difficult time in a complicated investigation that so few people understood…the waiting.

The proprietor turned to Pelleter with an ingratiating smile.

"So they found those boys." The proprietor shook his head. "They're too old to have gotten lost in a field," he said, and he snorted. "When I was their age, I had to walk miles just to milk the cows."

Pelleter did not reply, but there was a subtle relaxation of his shoulders. It was the first he had heard that the boys had been found, but he was not surprised. It accounted for the town's quiet. He reached for a cigar, then remembered he was about to have lunch, and dropped his hand.

"To cause so much trouble," the proprietor continued, "I hope they get a sound thrashing."

The waitress returned with Pelleter's sandwich, wrapped, he noticed with some satisfaction, in yesterday's *Vérité*.

"But how are they? Is everything okay? And this other thing with the dead prisoners and the missing girl?"

Pelleter ignored the proprietor's questions, making a point to say thank you to the waitress as he took his lunch.

Outside he took a long refreshing swallow of beer. The sandwich was good. Benoît, even in his crisis, made good bread, crisp and firm. He ate as he crossed the square, the sweat beginning again to pour down his back. It was good that the boys were safe, but he felt lost in this other thing. He could not help but feel as though he kept forgetting to do the simplest things that would lead him to the answer. There were too many distractions. He contemplated for a moment how a small town could seem to have more distractions than the city.

He saw the man standing in the shadow of the police station steps before he recognized him. "A happy ending, Monsieur Pelleter!"

"Servières."

"We're doing another special edition tonight. The headline…" He traced his open hand across the air. "*FOUND.*"

Pelleter continued to eat. "You really are becoming a daily."

"This may be my chance for a larger market."

"Then who would write the *Vérité*?"

"Inspector! It's good to see you in high spirits as well. I'm not the only reporter at the *Vérité*."

Pelleter finished his sandwich and made a point of balling up its wrapping, but Servières did not notice.

"What happened?"

Servières took out his notebook. Pelleter could not fight the feeling again that Servières was very much like him, and he felt a burst of warmth for the young reporter.

"Tuesday, April 4th at approximately five in the evening, Georges and Albert Perreaux left Monsieur Marque's sweet shop, and headed west on the Rue Principale on their way home to the Perreaux Farm.

"Georges decided it would be faster to cut across a field, but the boys quickly became lost, circling in the high grass in an ever-increasing panic."

"That's how you're going to write it?"

"I haven't settled on it yet. Dark fell, the rain started, and the boys were pinned down, lost in the field. In the morning, Albert was ill and unable to move. Georges was frightened to leave his brother.

"Madame Perreaux assumed that the boys had stayed with an aunt in town because of the weather and so she did not inform the police until Thursday, April 6th. Chief of Police Letreau organized an all-night search that continued into the morning until the boys were located in the field west of town, now both with fevers.

"They were removed to the hospital, and there will be more here with quotes from the police and the men who found them and maybe the boys themselves if I get lucky."

"Then why are you waiting out here?"

"Monsieur Rosenkrantz is inside, and I thought it best to stay out of his way, since it seems he's unhappy I mentioned his wife in yesterday's paper."

Pelleter smiled at that. He turned up the steps.

"Inspector, wait!"

Pelleter stopped, now looking down at Servières.

"Do you have anything new to report in the Meranger murder?"

Pelleter's smile softened.

"Or would you care to comment on the five prisoners' bodies that were found yesterday? Or Madame Rosenkrantz's disappearance?"

Pelleter's expression had turned dark, and he growled, "I thought you were running good news tonight, Servières."

"Good news is news that sells papers."

"Stick to the boys," Pelleter said and began to turn away. He stopped again.

"What is it?" Servières said.

Pelleter didn't reply. He thought again about how he felt as though he were forgetting something or some things and how he was at a loss as to what to do next, as he had thought that morning, that he was only reacting. Maybe the trick was to get something else to react to. He turned to Servières.

"Take this down. Inspector Pelleter is very encouraged about his investigation into the prisoners murdered at Malniveau Prison. He has some promising leads and hopes to have the case tied up by the time this paper goes to press tomorrow."

Servières was writing feverishly. When he finished he looked up at Pelleter, his eyes gleaming with excitement. "Is it true?"

"We'll know tomorrow, I guess." The chief inspector thought of the young, attractive woman standing in the entryway of the Verargent Hotel's dining room like a lost little girl. She did not need to be dragged through the papers. "And leave out Madame Rosenkrantz's disappearance."

"But everyone already knows—"

"Leave it out," Pelleter said, climbing the last step. "I gave you plenty." He pulled open the door to the police station at the back of Town Hall.

The police station was as deserted as the rest of the town, only it was as noisy as ever.

"You bastards search night and day when its two little boys missing, but you don't give a damn about a young woman!"

Monsieur Rosenkrantz was standing against the desk that separated the public space from the department offices. There were two police officers Pelleter did not recognize sitting at the desk furthest from Monsieur Rosenkrantz watching the angered man with silent determination. There was no one else in the office. Letreau had probably given everyone else leave for the rest of the day after last night's search.

Rosenkrantz was shouting in English now, and Pelleter was able to pick out more than one of the words he had learned in the war from an American soldier in return for teaching him the equivalents in French.

Pelleter came up behind the tall American, and slipped a hand under his elbow.

Rosenkrantz jerked away in surprise, but Pelleter had a tight grip.

"What are the police doing?" Rosenkrantz said, switching back to French. "Nobody's doing anything here. They searched night and day for those little boys. My wife's been missing for a day and a half now. Because of these two little miscreants, I haven't even been able to file a report."

"Come on," Pelleter said, nodding his head towards the chairs in the waiting area and tightening his grip on the American's elbow. "I'll see to you in a moment."

"Are you going to help me look for my wife?"

"Why don't we talk about it?"

Rosenkrantz regarded Pelleter for a moment. The two men were almost the same height, but Rosenkrantz managed to look down at Pelleter nevertheless. He pulled his arm away and Pelleter released it. "Okay. We'll talk."

The American straightened his overcoat, but did not sit down.

Pelleter went behind the desk and approached the two officers, whose expressions had not changed since Pelleter had come in, even now that the shouting had stopped. "Where's Chief Letreau?" Pelleter said, glancing into the chief of police's office.

"At the hospital with Madame Perreaux."

"Inspector!" Rosenkrantz called from the waiting area.

Pelleter held up his hand, and said to the officer, "And everyone else?"

"Skeleton crew until tomorrow. Don't want to pay us too much overtime."

The other officer tapped his companion on the shoulder, and the first officer realized what he had said.

"I mean, sir…"

"I know what you mean," Pelleter said. He turned.

"Any message, sir?" the second officer said.

"No."

"Inspector!"

As Pelleter approached Monsieur Rosenkrantz, he said, "Let's go."

The American writer said, "Where?"

"To talk about it," Pelleter said, taking out a cigar and busying himself with lighting it.

Rosenkrantz watched this performance, and then said curtly, "Okay. Fine." He turned and led the way out of the police station, and Pelleter followed.

Outside, the chief inspector was glad to see that Servières had had the sense to disappear. He was probably on his way to the hospital to try to get some quotes. Or perhaps he needed to go type up the chief inspector's comments immediately.

Rosenkrantz led them away from the square, into an area of town that appeared residential. He walked with long angry strides, his outrage far from gone, but for the moment invested in walking. At a small alley, no larger than one man across, he turned. The windows at ground level were all shuttered. Empty laundry lines crisscrossed between the buildings above their heads, each line just long enough for a single shirt or several socks.

Halfway down the alley there was a steep set of stairs, almost vertical. Rosenkrantz went down, holding the side of the building for support, guiding his head beneath the low passage and through a door.

Pelleter followed and found himself in a private pub, just a board across the width of the room held by evenly spaced posts acting as a bar. There were no tables. The place smelled of stale cigarette smoke and sour beer. Pelleter's shoes stuck to the floor, each step giving way with a resisting crack as he stepped up to the bar.

They were the only people there. The ancient barman had been sleeping on his stool with his head leaned against the wall, but he stood, rubbing his eyes when Rosenkrantz knocked on the board. He set two pints on the bar without either patron ordering.

Rosenkrantz stared ahead as he drank, still standing. The ceiling was only inches from the tops of their heads.

The barkeep went back to sleep in his corner.

Down in this basement, it was already night.

Pelleter took a seat and left his beer untouched. He watched Rosenkrantz drink, smoking his cigar and waiting for the man to speak. He remembered what Servières had said about Rosenkrantz's drinking bouts.

Half a pint gone, Rosenkrantz, still facing forward said, "Why would she have gone away?"

"You tell me."

Rosenkrantz turned. There was real hurt in his face. He shook his head. "She wouldn't have." He downed the rest of his beer, and turned to wake the barkeep, but Pelleter said, "Have mine."

Rosenkrantz took it, but he only held it. "I didn't know her father was in Malniveau until you showed up at our door. I knew he was in prison, of course, but it had never occurred to me that he was in our prison."

"She visited him there."

"How do you know?"

"She told me."

Rosenkrantz drank then.

"I know I'm an old man to her," Rosenkrantz said, setting the empty glass down. "That sometimes it must seem like I'm a father to her more than a husband. But I love her more than anything, more than my country, more than my writing."

He knocked on the bar, and the barkeep startled, then shuffled to refill their glasses.

"I can understand that people might keep secrets from each other, that's how I make my living, making up all of these little lies that people tell each other, but why keep this about her father? And why disappear without a word? She knows it would kill me."

He drank the newly poured beer.

"So you were never in communication with Meranger?"

"Never. I hated the man without having met him."

"And anyone else at the prison?"

Rosenkrantz motioned with his glass. "Here. In town. Maybe. But not to talk to. I don't really know anyone here, except Clotilde. That's why those bastards at the police department won't help me." His eyes opened wide. "That's why you have to help me. You have to find her. And prove…"

"Prove what?"

"Whatever it is that they say about her in the papers is wrong."

"The papers just said the murdered man was her father."

"That's already too much."

"You'll have to take that up with Philippe Servières."

Rosenkrantz finished his pint and began the second one without asking Pelleter if he wanted it. The writer was unsteady on his feet. He probably hadn't eaten since Madame Rosenkrantz disappeared, and he was drinking very fast.

The barkeep saw the mood that the American writer was in, and decided that he would not get any more sleep.

Rosenkrantz began to ramble, to tell of how he had met Clotilde and left his first wife, an American who still received half of his earnings in the States, and their son.

Five pints…six. Pelleter was not yet finished with his cigar.

He talked of how they had chosen to move to Verargent despite Hollywood's clamoring for him to come out there and work on a salary, and how he loved the solitude, the way that his whole world could be wrapped up in his writing and his wife.

The barkeep went to refill Rosenkrantz's glass, but Pelleter shook his head, and the barkeep pulled back.

Rosenkrantz turned to the chief inspector, almost falling. "Do you think she's all right? You don't think that whoever went for her father would also go for her?"

"I think she's fine," Pelleter said. "Come sit down."

"Is it true what they're saying about these other murdered prisoners?"

"What are they saying?"

"That there were other murdered prisoners."

"It's true."

Rosenkrantz went to lift his glass and noticed that it was empty. "More beer," he bellowed. "What are you thinking!"

The old man refilled the writer's glass, too timid to even cast an angry look at Pelleter.

The chief inspector said again, "Why don't you sit down?"

Seven pints…eight. Rosenkrantz at last sat down and put his head on the bar at once. His voice muffled, he said, "I just don't know what to do. They searched everywhere for those boys and no one found my wife. What do I do?"

The chief inspector called to the barkeep about a taxi.

"There's no phone in the house," the old man said.

Pelleter went out to get the taxi himself. The threatening clouds had broken up and were now thin white wisps against the darkening sky. Night was falling and with it, how many missed opportunities? How long before he could go back home to his own wife?

The taxi was in its usual place before the café, and when Pelleter explained what he needed, the driver knew the place at once. He had been called there many times.

It took all three men, even the old barkeep, to get Rosenkrantz up the steep stairs and down the alley. Once the American was in the back seat, Pelleter took his place beside the driver, and the barkeep went back to his pub.

Rosenkrantz had a tab. The barkeep would be paid in time.

When they reached the Rosenkrantz home, night had fallen. The other evening, huddled down as it had been against the storm, the house's charm had still come across, but now empty in the night, it just appeared lifeless and forlorn.

Pelleter stepped out of the car and thought he saw a shadow move at the end of the drive, just a darker patch of dark. He stepped towards the street without closing his car door, fixing his eyes on the spot. It could have just been a shrub moving in the breeze, or was somebody out there...following him? He continued along the drive, ignoring the sounds of the cabman behind him. The shape moved again, and then joined a hedge.

"Hey," the cabman shouted behind him. "A little help."

Pelleter continued towards the shadow, still peering into the darkness. He saw no more movement. Had it been Madame Rosenkrantz? No, she would have let herself into the house.

"Inspector!"

Pelleter held still, listening for sounds. "Come out now," he called. The bushes swayed in a faint breeze. Nothing. Was he overtired from the night before?

"Inspector!" the cabbie shouted again.

Pelleter turned back. If someone was following him, he would find out who and why soon enough.

The cabman was leaning into the back seat of the car, his silhouette lit by the dash as he struggled with Rosenkrantz's inert form.

The chief inspector came up alongside the taxi driver, and leaned in beside him, the two men shoulder-to-shoulder as they hoisted the unconscious American writer up off the seat and into the cool of the night. The rank smell of alcohol caused Pelleter to wince even more than the dead weight of the large man.

They shuffled up to the house, the taxi driver muttering the whole time, "Come on, you bastard, come on, you bastard, come on…"

At the door, Pelleter began to look for the writer's keys, but the driver tried the handle and found it open. Perhaps Rosenkrantz had been afraid that his wife would come home and not be able to get in. Perhaps, even with all of the excitement, it would not have occurred to the American to lock his door. After all, wasn't that one of the reasons they had moved to Verargent?

The two sober men turned sideways to manage the doorway, and Pelleter darted his eyes back to the street to the spot where he had seen the shadow. Sure enough it seemed again as though someone was out there. But Pelleter couldn't give chase until he'd set down the

American, so he just staggered forward. What had the chief inspector discovered that was reason for being followed?

Inside, the door swung slowly closed behind them. They labored in the darkness of the small hallway, dragging the writer between them.

"This way," the driver said at the first opening. Enough light came through the window to make out the shadow of an armchair. They deposited the drunken man, and Pelleter stretched, his hands at the small of his back, his heart racing from exertion.

"I should get paid extra for this," the driver said. His brusque voice seemed too loud in the darkness.

Pelleter reached into his pocket and pulled out some francs, handing them over without making out the denominations.

"He should pay."

Pelleter looked for a lamp. There was a gasoline sconce beside the door, which Pelleter lit with one of his matches, revealing a standard sitting room. "You go back. I'll be fine."

The driver shrugged. He had been driving the inspector all day, but he was not a curious man and it was getting near dinner. He left the room.

Pelleter stepped to the window. He knew it would make him visible to anyone who might be watching—the light behind him and the darkness outside—but that was fine. It might lure his tail into a false sense of security, that he could see but couldn't be seen. However, the only movement outside was the cabman reversing his car down the drive. As his headlights swept the hedge and the street, they revealed no one. The man who had been out there was probably long gone.

Pelleter turned around. He regarded the slumped form of Monsieur Rosenkrantz. Clotilde was loved if nothing else. And that was something. That was a lot.

The chief inspector took another look around the room. It was hardly used, much of the furniture brand new and the rug on the floor unmarked by footprints. The only thing that gave the room a feeling of habitation were the two built-in bookcases to either side of the fireplace jammed with books in French, English, and Spanish, two-deep in places. The liquor cart in the corner was devoid of liquor, the glasses in need of a dusting.

Out in the hall, the day's mail was still in a scattered pile on the floor. Pelleter picked it up, and flipped through. It was actually the last several days' mail: bills, airmail from the States, a printed envelope from a well-known magazine in the city. He set it on a sidetable in the entryway.

Across the way was a dining room that he could make out well enough in the light from the sitting room. It was a small room, the table filling the whole space. He went through, pushing into the kitchen, which was so dark that he lit another match, looking for a lamp. He found one hanging from the ceiling in the center of the room over a butcher block table. Clotilde kept her kitchen clean. The surfaces were all spotless, as was the floor. The drawers and cabinets were kept neatly, the silverware stacked, the pots and pans inside one another. There was a porcelain double sink with running water. It made sense that the American writer would be sure to provide his young bride with the luxuries that she would most appreciate.

There was a rear door to the kitchen that opened further along the main hallway. One door in the hall led to the back yard while another across the way revealed Rosenkrantz's study. He'd left a lamp burning on his desk, and it cast a glow on the room, revealing the disarray of papers and books in stacks on every surface including the floor. There were framed photographs of Clotilde on the desk, along with several older photographs of an elderly couple that must have been the writer's American parents.

Rosenkrantz and Clotilde did appear to be the content pair they seemed. They lived in isolated marital bliss. Clotilde had been troubled over her father's death, confused really, when Pelleter saw her. But she hadn't seemed frightened. There would have been no reason for her to run.

He forced his way to the small window between two of the bookcases, and looked between the blinds out into the back yard. There was nothing there to see. So his supposed tail, if there was one, was probably alone, which meant that he was effectively useless, two men required to follow someone successfully. There were too many players and it seemed that all of the important ones he couldn't see. He blew out the lamp on Rosenkrantz's desk before going back into the hall.

He went upstairs to be thorough, not expecting to find anything. The upstairs was a large single room with the staircase opening in the center of the floor, a railing around the other three sides of the opening. There was more light from the windows here than downstairs. The bed was unmade, and the armoire left opened, but these were the signs of an absent wife, not of a hurried departure. There was nothing to find here.

Pelleter went back downstairs without further investigation.

Rosenkrantz had not moved during Pelleter's search. His chest rose and fell with labored breaths. With luck he would be out for the rest of the night.

Pelleter left, feeling the front door latch behind him. The evening was clear and pleasant, an evening meant for enjoyment. As he reached the street, he listened for footsteps behind him, but heard nothing. At the first closed storefront with a display window, the chief inspector stopped as though to look inside, and glanced behind him, but there was no one there. If he had been followed earlier, he wasn't being followed now.

In the lobby of the hotel, Pelleter asked the girl at the desk to ring up headquarters for him. The missing children had distracted him. He should have gotten in touch with Lambert before this. Hopefully the lost time would not prove too costly.

The girl left for a moment and when she returned she said the call would be put through directly.

He asked for a newspaper and told her that he was ready to take his dinner.

She pulled a fresh copy of the *Vérité* from under the counter, and then came around and disappeared into the dining room.

Pelleter didn't watch her go. His eyes were fixed on the headline:

### FOUND!

Of course Servières could not leave it as a simple story. He placed emphasis on the fact that the boys had been found by two civilians, not gendarmes, and he cast aspersions on the effectiveness of Chief Letreau and the local police department given the recent rash of crime. Yes, he was making his bid for a larger market. Stirring up trouble was a good way to do it.

Pelleter flipped through the rest of the two-sheet paper and stopped at the article on the Meranger murders. As of right now, the *Vérité* was not committing to the idea that Meranger's murder was connected to the five murdered prisoners from the field. They had been found in different places after all, and in different circumstances. The *Vérité*, however, was encouraged to find that visiting Chief Inspector Pelleter of the Central Bureau was very optimistic about the case, having uncovered a promising new lead that he would follow up immediately.

There was no mention of Madame Rosenkrantz's disappearance. Pelleter hoped that Monsieur Rosenkrantz would appreciate that he had done that much for him. He was pleased that Servières had gone along with his ploy. Now the inspector would have to think of something to back it up with in the morning.

He turned to go into the dining room, and he saw out of the corner of his eye that there was a man sitting in an armchair in the corner, a second before the man said, "Chief Inspector."

The inspector turned fully then.

The man sat with his right ankle on his left knee. The same newspaper was spread out in his lap. His suit, as always, was impeccable.

"I think we need to have a talk," Fournier said.

# 9.

## *The Assistant Warden*

Pelleter realized that Fournier must have been waiting for him since before he arrived, which meant that the assistant warden had been able to watch the inspector turn through the paper unobserved. Pelleter had done nothing inappropriate, but he was still rankled at being caught unawares. There was nothing to be done about it now.

"Yes," he said, and with a false bow, he invited Fournier into the dining room. "Let's talk."

Fournier refolded the paper, taking care to pull at the end of each crease so that when he was finished the paper appeared brand new. He stood, left the paper on the seat, and led the way into the dining room.

Once inside, Pelleter took his seat so that he faced the door, and spread his napkin in his lap as though he were simply sitting down to dinner. He looked uninterested, a man at the end of an exhausting workday, when in reality he was watching Fournier's every movement.

The assistant warden took the seat opposite, where Clotilde-ma-Fleur Rosenkrantz had sat two nights before. His face was set, as though he were determined to say what he had come to say without being waylaid.

As he prepared himself, the girl from the counter approached behind him.

Fournier began, "You can not come and go as you please at the prison. It's unacceptable!"

"Monsieur Inspector?"

Fournier jumped, and turned in his seat to see the girl who was leaning in towards them with her hands clasped.

"The phone…"

"Ah, yes," Pelleter said, bunching up his napkin. "You'll excuse me, Monsieur Fournier, of course. It'll only be a moment." Pelleter stood, pushing back his seat, and extracting himself from the table. "And you should let the chef know that it will be two of us for dinner."

Fournier looked frightened by this sudden turn of events, looking at the girl and then Pelleter and then the girl again. "No, I'm not staying for dinner."

"Of course you are. You've had a very trying few days, after all. I won't be a minute."

Fournier's fear had converted to frustrated anger, but Pelleter passed out of the dining room, and went to the phone that had been left on the front desk for him.

He picked up the receiver:

"Lambert? It's me…Yes, I need you to locate somebody for me…" He gave the name. "Check the hotels… He's with his wife, so he shouldn't be hiding too carefully…Call me when you've found him, either at the hotel or through Letreau. But don't lose sight of him…Very good…Yes."

He hung up, and went back into the dining room.

Fournier was sitting facing forward, his back to the door. He sat up straight, his shoulders squared. Pelleter spoke before Fournier could see him, but the assistant warden did not act startled. He'd regained his composure.

"Sorry about that. The telephone must not be ignored. Never know when it's going to be something important. Or when you'll be able to get in touch with the other person again, the chances of you both being at the phone at the same time..." He resumed his seat, and replaced his napkin. He continued to ramble, setting a nonchalant, jovial tone, knowing that it would further anger Fournier and make the man more likely to make a mistake. "Perhaps it's best to communicate through telegraph, but a telegraph can be too easy to ignore, so...here we are. You were saying?"

Fournier pressed his lips together, and exhaled through his nose. In a tight voice, he said, "You can not come—"

"Oh, yes, I can not come and go as I please at the prison. Well I had an escort, and I was told you were busy."

"That's beside the point. The prison must remain secure, and to do that, certain rules must be followed."

"Ah, of course," Pelleter said, remaining offhand. "Where were you today, by the way?"

"The results of our search turned up many things that had to be dealt with even if it didn't turn up the knife used to cut our prisoner. Running a prison is complicated enough without outside forces meddling. For instance, you can not have your man at the prison. That too is unacceptable."

"My man?"

"Going through our files."

"Well, it's not my man. It's Letreau's. You must take it up with him."

Fournier scoffed. "Letreau? The chief of police is adequate at his job, but this is a small town, and his job does not ask much of him. Everybody knows that you are running this investigation."

"But it was Letreau who sent the officer to Malniveau."

Fournier clenched his teeth. His eyes lit with anger. "I will not—"

The proprietor appeared then with two steaming plates of ratatouille. "Ah, here you are, Chief Inspector, and Monsieur Fournier, what a pleasure to have you. You will love this, I am sure. *Bon appetit! Bon appetit!*"

He set a plate down before each man, and clapped his hands together. There was a pause, and then he edged away from the table.

Pelleter took up his silverware. "What's the problem with *my* man?"

"He's distracting my staff, and interfering with my systems. I can't have an outsider requesting to see every piece of paper we have produced in the last two months."

Good boy, Martin, Pelleter thought. He was the right choice for the job. He has shown more big-city pluck than any of the others. I have to be sure he gets back out there first thing in the morning.

"I told you earlier, if you insist that we're all in this together then you must trust that I will come forward with anything I find."

"Then can you tell me what you know of the five prisoners who were buried in a farm field ten miles from the prison?" Pelleter said. He took a bite of his meal after this quiet question, but his eyes didn't leave Fournier's face.

"What! I will not be mocked. Surely you're not serious."

With the same calm, Pelleter said, "I am serious." He

reached into his pocket, took out his notebook and flipped it open to the page with the five prisoner numbers on it, and slid it across the table. "You haven't heard about this yet?"

Fournier glanced at the numbers without touching the notebook. "I don't know anything about it."

Pelleter took another bite of his food, but still watched Fournier. The assistant warden's anger had shifted away from Pelleter and broadened, as he looked off to the side, thinking. It seemed as though he were genuinely surprised at this discovery. He *was* isolated out at the prison. And it seemed he did not know everything that went on there either.

The assistant warden turned back to the inspector. "When was this done? Perhaps this was from years ago…"

What he meant was, before his time. "In the last few weeks."

Fournier looked to the side again. When he turned back to the inspector, his anger had dissipated, and he was now conspiratorial. "You must understand…the warden…" He paused, and Pelleter could see him struggle with his political self, trying to decide if it was yet time to speak out against his superior. "The warden started his career as a guard at Malniveau. He did his time, his years pacing those corridors, standing watch with a shotgun, sitting in a cold guard box alone for hours. He didn't go to school. He's never been out of Verargent for more than the occasional trip to the city or the seashore. For him, the prisoners are the enemy to be controlled, and that's it.

"And they are! I don't disagree, but there's more to

that than violence and a show of force…I studied administration. I worked in the private sector for an importer,
overseeing shipments, arranging transport. Everything
had to be planned in advance, calculated on paper—the
paperwork! And the reality of it all had to be addressed,
of the people out there on the boats or on the docks, real
people, you understand. Real people.

"All of these things are the same in a prison. The prisoners are people. But they are also the things that must
be transported, stored, maintained. That means paperwork. And diligence. And understanding."

He was really opening up now. Pelleter had fallen
silent, not wishing to interfere with the assistant warden's
confession. And Fournier took that silence as a sympa-
thetic invitation. They were both in law enforcement,
after all. Pelleter understood.

"The warden is all violence and might," Fournier said.
"He has no finesse."

"Are you saying the warden killed these men?" Pelleter
said suddenly, leaning forward.

Fournier looked confused. "No," he said, shaking his
head. "The warden? No, he's not a murderer…"

Pelleter sat back, and took another bite of his ratatouille. He was almost finished with it.

"I'm simply saying the warden is incompetent. That
you have no idea what work I have had to do to get
things in order, and I have had to fight at every step. We
need a form for this. We need a form for that. And the
warden always resists. But then things slip between the
cracks." He raised his hand and let it fall on the table in
frustration.

Pelleter pushed back his dish. "Like people getting counted present, when they are missing."

"For example," Fournier said, and sneered.

Pelleter waited in silence to see if the assistant warden would say more.

Fournier renewed his vigor. "You can not push me around. I've worked in the city, and I worked my way up at two other national prisons." He stopped, sitting up in his seat. He had not touched the food in front of him. He felt empowered by recounting his story. "Call off your man."

Pelleter took a cigar from his pocket, and took the time to light it. He blew out the smoke, which hung over the table between them. Then, in a quiet, deliberate voice, he said, "How did Meranger get out of the prison?"

Fournier, surprised by the question, exploded, "I don't know! I'm doing everything—"

"Not enough!" Pelleter barked, and the benevolent confessor was gone, as was the babbling fool from the beginning of the meal.

Fournier for all of his bluster, blanched at Pelleter's quiet indignation. "Are you accusing me of being involved?"

"It had crossed my mind," Pelleter said.

Fournier looked down at his untouched meal, and then out through the thin curtain, and then into the empty dining room, unable to settle his gaze. At last, he looked back at Pelleter, and he was seething, his anger from earlier nothing compared to the white anger that was paralyzing his body. "How dare you," he managed, choking on the words.

Pelleter blew a plume of smoke, calm and dismissive.

Fournier pushed back from the table, almost knocking over his chair, which was only saved from falling by the chair behind. He righted it, and then stormed across the room, and out the door. A moment later, a car could be heard as it started and screeched around the square, the man still controlled by his outrage.

Pelleter sat, enjoying his cigar, the air above him filling with smoke. Verargent was quiet, a small town after dark.

In his room with the lights off, Pelleter could not sleep, despite the physical activity of the afternoon and evening.

Fournier had been genuinely surprised when Pelleter had told him of the five murdered prisoners found in the field. If Meranger constituted a sixth murder, and the man stabbed the day before was meant to be a seventh… Well, it stood to reason that somebody was committing the murders inside the prison. The real question was the one that Mahossier had put to Pelleter and Pelleter had put to Fournier and was now putting to himself over and over:

How were the dead men removed from the prison without anybody knowing?

Or the other way to ask that was, Who was removing the dead prisoners from the prison without anybody else knowing?

Because Pelleter was certain that Meranger had been killed within the prison walls as well. And if Fournier truly knew nothing…

He tried to remember everyone who he had seen in his three trips to the prison, but there were too many to recall, and he had not seen everybody. That was definitely the case: he had not seen everybody.

His mind turned the facts round and round, and then at some point, as he asked himself again who had moved Meranger, he fell asleep.

# 10.

## A Lineup

Pelleter had not taken two steps out of the Hotel Verargent the next morning when he was accosted on the street.

"Inspector Pelleter! Were you happy with my article? Another special edition, no less."

It was Philippe Servières.

Pelleter turned towards the police station without even casting a glance towards the reporter. The town was busy with early morning activity. People who worked in the businesses in town hurried to their jobs, while housewives who liked to do their shopping early already carried parcels. Two senior citizens had taken up their place on the shaded side of the war monument.

It all seemed quite normal. Pelleter had seen small towns like this in a panic once an article like Servières' came out, but it had had no serious effect. Perhaps they viewed it as a prison problem, something outside of town.

Servières hurried two steps to fall in beside Pelleter. "We're doing another special today. This is big news. Do you want anything else to go into the paper? Do you think we can help flush out the murderer?"

Pelleter walked with quick assurance, ignoring the reporter. He had awoken with an idea that he was eager to put into effect, something to support his claims in the

paper, and it felt good to be on the move, acting instead
of reacting.

"I need to keep the story alive. I can't keep the Rosenkrantz girl's disappearance out of it forever. Inspector, a
comment?"

They were outside Town Hall now, a police car parked
out front. Pelleter turned the corner towards the police
station.

"It seems to me," Servières went on, "that the only
reason Madame Rosenkrantz had to run off was because
she killed her father. And that your lack of interest in
finding her is a gross failure."

Pelleter turned back then, already on the steps to the
station so that he towered over Servières. Servières fell
back, surprised and off guard.

"Is that what you're going to say in the paper?" Pelleter
said.

Servières' assurance had vanished. "Well, yes."

"You may want to think twice about that. Monsieur
Rosenkrantz will be very unhappy."

"I don't print things to make people happy. I print the
news."

"But this is just your opinion," Pelleter said, and turned
away, going into the police station, and leaving Servières
cowed on the steps.

The station was in direct opposition to the sunny calm
outside. Martin was back at the front desk. The woman
with the yappy dog had returned, dog in hand, another
poor driver accused of attempted canine slaughter, the
yelling parties handled by two officers. Pelleter was surprised to see that Monsieur Rosenkrantz stood in front of

one of the other desks, shouting over the noise at one of the officers who had assisted Pelleter with the coffins.

When Rosenkrantz saw Pelleter, he walked over, leaving the officer who was taking his statement behind. "She still hasn't turned up," Rosenkrantz said.

"Sir?" the officer said. "I'll help you."

"You seem steadier on your feet this morning."

"I'm beside myself with panic."

"This officer will take your statement," Pelleter said, inviting Rosenkrantz to turn back around.

"These officers should have taken my statement days ago! She's disappeared. She could be dead somewhere, but what are they doing? Looking after dogs and children! Someone killed her father, why not kill her too? Wipe out the whole family. This is what you should be working on."

"Sir?"

Pelleter readjusted his stance. "That's the second theory I've heard already today. The first was that your wife killed her father and then ran off."

"Who said that?"

"Have you checked with the conductor? Has she taken a train?"

"I checked. She hasn't. Who said she killed her father?"

"And the car?"

"I have it. But she could have hitchhiked out of town. That doesn't mean anything. I think she's been murdered. Now who's saying this other nonsense?"

The officer who had been taking Rosenkrantz's statement gave up, and sat back down at his desk.

"Servières. He's going to put it in the *Vérité*. He's right outside."

Rosenkrantz scowled. "I'll..." he started, and then hurried through the front door.

"Good work," Pelleter said, smiling at the officer at the desk.

The yappy dog barked, the sound cutting through the small station.

Letreau appeared at the door to his office. He looked haggard, as though he had not slept the night before, his hair out of place and his clothes wrinkled. "What is going on out here?"

Pelleter went over to Martin, taking his oilcloth notebook from his pocket.

Letreau saw the inspector, and joined him at the front desk, but when the dog barked again, he turned and yelled, "Get that animal out of here!"

The woman holding the dog immediately turned her tirade on Letreau who found himself pulled into the argument.

Pelleter had Martin copy the prisoner numbers from his notebook. It was obvious from the care that Martin took making the notes that he was proud to have been singled out by the inspector for this task. When he finished writing the numbers, he looked up at Pelleter expectantly, like a disciple given precious time with the master.

"I want you to go back to the prison," Pelleter said. "Look up everything there is on these five prisoners. Check Meranger too. See if there's anything unusual in the files."

Letreau rejoined them. "It's been like this all morning. Rosenkrantz left?"

"I sent him after Servières."

Letreau tilted his head in a confused question.

Pelleter patted him on the shoulder. "It's going to be all right. We're on the path now."

This made Letreau only shake his head in disbelief. "I don't know what you're talking about."

Martin was still looking up at Pelleter, waiting for more orders.

Pelleter nodded his head towards the door. "Go on."

Martin clambered to his feet.

Pelleter stopped him. "And tell Fournier I'll be out there shortly, and that he should have all of his men available to me, even those who are not on duty. I want them all out there."

Martin waited a beat to see if there was going to be anything else, and then he rushed out the door.

"Now, I'm really confused," Letreau said. "You're ordering my men?"

"I hope you don't mind. I've got an idea, and I'm ready to put it to the test. We'll head out to the prison shortly."

"Back to the prison?"

"Come, let's walk by the baker's house first."

Letreau shook his head. "You really are ahead of me. Between this and the children, I haven't been able to get a moment's rest, and you look happier than a kid on Christmas."

"Well, we still have to see. We still have to see. How are the children?"

"Marion…Madame Perreaux…is in a worse state than they are. The boys just have a fever. Nothing a few days in bed won't cure."

"Good," Pelleter said, his expression serious. "Good."

Outside, the weather was the kind of inviting spring weather that fell into the background just because it was so perfect. Verargent continued to look like a picturesque town, a completely different place than the rain-drenched community that Pelleter had found when he first arrived.

Before they had even left the square, Monsieur Benoît appeared.

"Inspector. Chief. Something must be done about this... Everyone wants to hear how I found the body. There is a crowd in my store."

"That's good," Letreau said.

"Yes. Good." The baker hunched his shoulders, and his eyes wandered to the side. "But I know how this is. If you don't find the murderer, then soon my name will be the only one attached to this thing, and people will think of my store and they'll think of a dead body, and then business will be bad, very bad."

Pelleter said, "We are on our way to your house now, for another look at where you found the body. We're taking care of this. It will all get resolved."

Benoît looked at Letreau. "Yes?"

Letreau said, "Enjoy the extra business. Doesn't your wife need your help?"

Benoît looked behind him, back towards his store. "Yes," he said, nodding. "Yes." He paused. "And you will find this murderer. My name..." He didn't wait for an answer, but turned and rushed back towards his store.

Letreau shook his head when he left. "The whole town is crazy."

Pelleter didn't respond, but started north.

"I thought you already examined the baker's street when you searched for the Perreaux children."

"I did."

"Then what do you expect to find?"

Pelleter smiled, lighting a cigar. "Fresh air and pleasant company."

Pelleter walked on. His principal purpose was to give Martin time to get to the prison so that Fournier could round up his men. The assistant warden had made an effort the night before. It was only fair to give him warning this time.

They came to Benoît's house. In the intervening days, the street had returned to what it had always been, simply a quiet residential street. A stranger to the town walking by this spot would never know that only days before a man's body had been found here in the gutter. There was nothing to see.

Pelleter smoked his cigar as he paced the street, observing the ground, and the houses around just in case there was something he had missed. If his plan didn't work, he could always interrogate all of the neighbors to see if they had seen anything that night. But it had to work. He had gone to sleep wondering how Meranger had gotten out of the prison, and he woke up even more convinced that if he could answer that, then he'd have the whole thing.

He continued to pace and smoke until he had smoked his entire cigar. Then he looked up and said, "Okay."

"Did you find anything?" Letreau said.

He nodded as though the trip had been very fruitful. Then he looked at Letreau. "Let's go to the prison."

The now familiar sight of Malniveau rose up before them. The sunny weather might light the walls, but it did little to make the prison appear other than what it was, a dreary place for the confinement of souls.

They waited for the outer guard to open the main gate.

"I don't understand why we're here," Letreau said. "Martin can handle going through paperwork well enough on his own."

"We're not here to go through paperwork," Pelleter said, staring straight ahead as the inner courtyard was revealed through the opening gate. "We're here to have a lineup."

Letreau inched the car forward, and the walls of the prison closed around them. There were more vehicles parked in the small courtyard than there had been on their previous visits, and Letreau had to maneuver the car along one of the walls and onto a small patch of crabgrass.

"You can't really expect to interrogate all of the prisoners," Letreau said, getting out of the car.

"Not the prisoners."

A look of understanding softened the features of Letreau's face. Then he frowned. "Fournier's not going to like that."

"That's why I gave him some time to get used to the idea."

Inside, Fournier was not happy to see them at all. He could not bring himself to look at Pelleter, forgetting himself one moment, and then hurriedly averting his eyes the next, using his ever-present clipboard as a shield.

Pelleter outlined his plan. "I want to interrogate each and every one of the prison workers—the guards, the infirmary staff, the office workers, the cafeteria people, everyone. We'll take them one at a time. The room where I saw Mahossier on Wednesday should be fine. Just line them up outside."

"This is an insult to my people," Fournier said, looking at his clipboard. "And a disruption to the entire prison."

"At least one of your people has something to do with this. It's the only way the dead prisoners could get transported out of the building."

"I still don't understand how there could be dead prisoners I don't know about."

"But there are, so let's get started."

"When the warden…"

Pelleter raised his eyebrows at this, and Fournier didn't finish. The assistant warden waited another moment to show that he wasn't being bullied, and then he set off to make the arrangements.

A guard let Pelleter and Letreau into the interrogation room. An extra chair was brought from another room, and the inspector and the chief of police sat side by side on one side of the table, leaving the chair across from them blank. Pelleter put his notebook and pencil on the table in front of him, opened to a new page, but he didn't reach for it once the interrogations began.

"Please, sit down," Pelleter said, to the guard who had led them in.

The guard looked confused, and he checked behind him to see if somebody else was standing there.

Pelleter indicated the chair, and nodded his head. "Might as well start with you."

The guard rubbed his palms on his pants legs, and then sat down heavily in the chair across the way, slouching in the seat with his legs spread under the table. He looked at a point just to the right of the inspector's head.

Once the inspector began, his questions came quickly, his expression serious.

"What's your name?" Pelleter asked.

"Jean-Claude Demarchelier."

"How long have you worked at Malniveau prison?"

"Since I got out of school."

Pelleter raised his eyebrows.

"Three years."

"Do you like it here?"

The guard shrugged. "It's a job."

"But they don't pay you enough."

The guard shrugged again.

"Perhaps you look to make a little extra money on the side. Help get things for the prisoners. Maybe help hide things that need to be hidden."

The guard looked directly at Pelleter then, shaking his head in wide sweeps. "No. Never. Nothing like that. I just do my job, and go home. That's it."

"But when you're asked to do something you know is against the rules, you help out. Maybe it's an important person asking you. Fournier. The warden. You don't want to lose your job."

"Never," the guard said, and he looked at Letreau for help, to confirm what he was saying, but the chief of police sat impassive, watching. The guard looked to the door. It had been left open. Then he looked back at his interrogators. "I just do my job." His expression was pleading. It looked as though it would not take much to make him cry.

"Okay, you can go."

The guard sat for a moment, unsure if he had heard correctly. Then he sighed, and got up. He started for the door, but Pelleter stopped him.

"Before you go, just write your name down in this notebook."

The guard turned back, and he bent over the table in order to write. His handwriting was large, like a schoolboy in elementary school. He finished hurriedly, and left.

Letreau turned to Pelleter. "Do you really think that you're going to find anything this way? He could have been lying."

"He wasn't lying."

"How do you know?"

"I know."

"This could be a big waste of time. Maybe we should be looking for Madame Rosenkrantz. Benoît is right. It'll only be a matter of time before the town grows nervous with the thing."

"Call in the next person."

Letreau stood up, and went to the door. He came back with another guard. When he sat down, he leaned over to Pelleter and whispered in his ear, "They're lined up all the way down the hall."

That interrogation went much the same way as the first, as did the next one, and the one after that. Pelleter found a rhythm, and he asked the same questions again and again, even if he adjusted his tone and manner to fit each of the people he was interrogating. Soon the list on his notepad extended to a second column.

Fournier came by once, and he stood in watching some of the interrogations from behind the inspector. But soon after, he left, and Pelleter continued to have prison employee after prison employee brought in. He thought once that he might have found something, and he pushed, but it was only that the man brought in cigarettes for some of the prisoners. One of the cafeteria workers admitted to bringing home some of the food to feed her family and cut back on grocery costs.

None of them responded to the question of whether or not a superior had asked them to do something against the rules. Everyone had a different opinion about the number of prisoners who had been stabbed and how many had actually been killed.

After four hours, Pelleter held up his hand for a break.

"I told you this would get us nowhere."

"On the contrary."

"You think that you've learned something from this?"

"How many more are out there?"

"A lot? At least thirty."

"Then we're not done."

Pelleter lit a cigar, and took several puffs in contemplative silence. He glanced at the notebook on the table with the varied handwriting covering the page. Another list of names. So many names, but none of them were the right one.

The smoke from his cigar floated to the ceiling and

formed a cloud with the smoke from his previous cigars. The interrogations were exhausting, but he was convinced that he would find something. One of these people had to know something about removing the bodies. He just had to find which one.

He waved to Letreau to let the next one in. Letreau brought in a young guard, and they each took their respective seats. The guard was no more than twenty-two, and the scruff that he must have considered a beard was still patchy in parts, the space under his lower lip completely bald.

"What's your name?" Pelleter began.

"Jean Empermont."

Pelleter frowned. "You're the guard who marked Meranger as present the morning after he was killed."

The man looked down at his hands, which were in his lap. "Yes," he said, almost so quietly as to not be heard.

# 11.

## Getting Somewhere

Fournier had said that the man had been reprimanded, and Pelleter would not have been surprised to find that Fournier knew all too well how to dress a man down. He softened his tone.

"How long have you worked here?"

The man was slow to answer, and at first it seemed as though he might not. At last, still looking at his hands, he said, "It will be a year next month."

"And before this?"

"Nothing…I tried university, but I was no good at it… I helped my father with his painting business…then this."

All the time the man had not looked up. Here was a man who was familiar with failure. Who, in his short years, had tried his hand at several things, but always seemed plagued by ill-luck. He no doubt felt as though this new failure would soon lead to his termination, an action for which Fournier was no doubt simply awaiting the warden's return, and that he would once again be forced to make a fresh start of things.

Pelleter sat forward, eager but also gentle. "Can you tell me what happened Wednesday morning?"

"Nothing!" the man burst out. Then he looked up to see what effect this ejaculation had had, panicked that he had damaged his case by showing his exasperation.

"Nothing," he repeated quietly, his eyes pleading. He took a deep breath. "Each guard is responsible for roll call on his cell block. But it's almost a formality in the mornings because where would the prisoners have gone? I guess they could have died."

He stopped short, realizing what he had said.

Letreau shifted in his seat beside Pelleter, but the inspector stayed still, watching the guard intently.

He started again, holding his hands palm up. "We don't even let them out of their cells at that point. Each guard has a list, and he walks along the block, calling the names, and the prisoners respond. Then you mark them as here. I guess we're supposed to look through the windows, but nobody does. I went along the block. I called Meranger. Somebody said, 'Here,' and I marked him as present."

"They said it from inside the cell?"

"I thought so." He dropped his hands to his sides, and shook his head. "I don't know."

"Who told you to mark him as here?"

"No one."

"Fournier?"

The guard shook his head, confused. "No. No one. Somebody said here. It was just like every day."

"The warden?"

Letreau coughed suddenly, and turned in his seat.

"No." The guard's eyes were wide. "No. He said, here. I marked him here."

"Okay," Pelleter said, and sat back. He put his cigar in his mouth, but found that it was no longer burning. He tapped the gray bud of ash from the end of the cigar onto the floor.

"Okay?"

"Oh. Write your name on the notebook, and let in the next person." Pelleter was relighting his cigar.

The guard reached for the notebook as though he were waiting for some kind of trap. But as he wrote, Pelleter looked off into the distance, as though he had already forgotten that the man was there. The guard left on silent feet.

"Pelleter—" Letreau started, but the next guard had already come in.

He was a large man—over six foot—and older than most of the other men they had seen so far, at least as old as the inspector, with hair graying at the temples. He sat up straight in the chair, pushing out his broad chest over his rounded belly, and met Pelleter's eyes. "I've got nothing to say," he said.

Letreau noticed that Pelleter's manner changed. The inspector's movements, already slow, grew slower, and his eyelids dropped halfway. "How about your name? Will you say that?"

The guard sucked in his lower lip, and resettled his bulk on his chair. "Passemier."

"How long have you worked here?"

"Thirty-two years."

Pelleter raised his eyebrows and nodded. "Impressive."

"I've been here longer than most."

"But not the warden," Pelleter said. "He got his start here as well."

"We started together. We've been here the same amount of time."

"How come you're not warden?"

Passemier shifted, pressing his lips together. He paused before answering, weighing what he had already said versus what he was going to say. "We can't all be the warden. The warden's a good man. A great friend."

Pelleter turned the notebook towards himself. There was apparently something very interesting there all of a sudden that was more pressing than the interview.

Passemier waited him out, not saying anything.

"So you don't know anything about any of this?" Pelleter said, still looking at the notebook, although he wasn't reading a single line there. All of his energy was focused on the guard.

"Any of what?"

"Any of this?" Pelleter pushed back the notebook, and looked at the old guard.

"Meranger?" the man said, squinting. He brought a hand to his chin.

Pelleter made a gesture with his hand, but it was impossible to tell what it meant.

Passemier resumed his self-assured military pose. "Nothing."

"Okay," Pelleter said. He picked up the notebook and turned to a fresh page. "If you could just write your name here…"

"Okay?" The guard looked surprised. He had been prepared to get grilled. He glanced at Letreau and then back at Pelleter. "That's it?"

"You have nothing to say. You don't know anything about this. You're a long-standing guard here. What more can I ask?"

The guard shrugged, and his whole figure loosened

up, the weight of his stomach pulling his shoulders forward. He reached for the outstretched notebook and pencil, and held the notebook in hand while he wrote instead of setting it down on the table. When he finished he set it down, sighed, looked at both men again, and then stood by pushing his hands against his thighs.

When he was at the door, Pelleter said, "One last thing... How many stabbings would you say there have been in the prison this month."

"Seven," Passemier said, his hand on the doorknob.

"Is that a lot?"

Passemier shrugged. "It's happened before. But it's not usual."

"Thank you. No one else was sure."

Passemier nodded, and stepped out into the hall.

"You think he knows something," Letreau said as soon as they were alone.

"I know he knows something," Pelleter said, smoking again. "He knows that there were seven stabbings. No one else guessed more than four."

"So what now?"

"We continue."

But as the remainder of the employees filtered in one by one, Pelleter seemed disinterested, eager to get through them so that he could move on. He allowed Letreau to question some of them. Letreau followed the same method that he had seen Pelleter use all morning, and Pelleter would step in if he thought that something was missing. But no one else excited the same interest.

In the administrative office, Pelleter went directly to

Martin, who had indeed been given the desk in the corner that Pelleter had spotted the day before. He had stacks of files spread out before him.

"So?" Pelleter said.

Martin handed him a small stack of six folders without saying anything. The top one was Meranger. At the end of the file it said that Meranger had been transferred to the National Prison at Segré.

He went through the other five folders. They were the men who had been found in the field. They too had each been transferred to the National Prison at Segré.

"Good," Pelleter said, and handed the files to Letreau, so he could see.

"There is no national prison at Segré," Martin said, still seated and looking up at the inspector.

"I know."

"My god," Letreau said.

Pelleter stepped over to one of the nearest desks and picked up the telephone. He waited while he was connected.

Fournier arrived then. "Are you satisfied, now that you've terrorized my staff?"

Pelleter turned his back on the assistant warden, and spoke into the phone.

"Who is he calling?" Fournier said to Letreau, annoyed that the inspector was ignoring him.

"I don't know," Letreau said.

Pelleter hung up then. "Good. How's our stabbing victim from yesterday?"

Fournier seemed put off by this question. He had been expecting something else. "He's fine."

"Good. We'll see you later, I hope."

"Wait one second. What's going on?"

Pelleter turned to Martin. He showed him his note-book. "Pull these two files. Then go through all of the employee records. I want to know anyone else who started at the same time and is still on staff." Pelleter paused for a moment. Then he added, "Or was on staff until recently."

Martin stepped off.

Fournier sputtered. "I demand that you tell me what is going on."

Pelleter smiled, and it seemed to only make Fournier angrier. "Soon," Pelleter said. "When the first train arrives in the morning. We're almost done now."

Pelleter turned to Letreau, and then headed for the front door. Letreau fell in behind him.

Fournier called behind him, "Wait!"

Pelleter said, "We'll let you know."

Then he and Letreau went out to the car, which was just then in a bright ray of sunshine.

# 12.

## Madame Rosenkrantz is Found

It was dusk when they reached the police station in Verargent. As always, the town in evening was a shadow of its daytime self. The square was deserted. The lights in the café, the hotel, and a few other buildings were the only indication that the town was more than a stage set.

"You must join us for dinner tonight," Letreau said, slamming the police car's door. "My wife's appalled that I've let you take dinner by yourself through all this."

Pelleter met Letreau at the front of the car. "I haven't eaten alone yet. If people know where I am, they can reach me."

Letreau shook his head. He looked worn out, the lines in his forehead deeper than usual, his cheeks lax, pulling his eyes down. "Do you really have this thing nearly wrapped up? Because I don't see it."

"Some of it. We'll see what I actually know in the morning."

Letreau studied the inspector's face to see if he could read the solution there. He sighed, and dropped his hand on Pelleter's shoulder. "You're sure about dinner?"

"I want to go for a little walk now," Pelleter said. "But thank your wife."

Letreau shook his head. "You're not making things

easy for me." He laughed, but it was strained, his face muscles tight. He dropped his hand, nodded, seemed as though he was going to say something else, nodded again, and then went up the station steps. At the top of the steps, he turned, hand on the door, and called, "First thing in the morning." Then he disappeared into the station.

Pelleter wanted to check on something before he returned to his hotel. He walked away from the square.

The streetlamps had been lit, and the light from the houses cast a pale glow into the night. The evening had a safe coziness to it proper to the town, and it was hard to imagine that Verargent could ever feel unsafe. When he came to the hospital, the extra light from the building seemed harsh and unnecessary.

The hospital was a single-story structure that had been built at what was once the outskirts of town, but was now embedded in the town proper. The building was simple and functional, which made it appear institutional even from the outside.

Pelleter went inside. A nurse sat at a desk just inside the door, reading the new special edition of the *Verargent Vérité*. Its headline simply read, "Murder!", which meant that Rosenkrantz had been very convincing when he spoke to Servières about not mentioning his wife in the paper.

"May I help you?" the nurse said, looking up.

"I'm Inspector Pelleter. I've come to look in the morgue."

"We don't have a morgue. More of an all-purpose storage room in the back. But they've sure filled it up with bodies this week…Take that door there. That's the men's ward…There are double doors straight back, which lead into a hall…The first door in front of you will be the storage room."

The ward had twelve beds along each of the longer walls. There were windows lining the outer wall, but the inner wall was a solid partition separating the men's ward from the women's. It didn't extend to the ceiling.

Only eight of the beds were occupied, two of them by children, both asleep. Pelleter stopped and looked at the boys. They must have been the Perreaux brothers. It was amazing that such little forms could stir up so much trouble. The chief inspector's mind turned involuntarily to the fate he had imagined for these two boys when it seemed as though Mahossier could have them. He looked away. A nurse was distributing dinners from a cart in the center aisle. Pelleter went on.

No one paid attention to the chief inspector as he went through to the doors at the back of the room. The hallway there lined the rear of the building with evenly spaced doors down the length of the hall. One door was open at the center of the hall, and a radio could be heard playing a slow jazz song.

Pelleter opened the door to the makeshift morgue and was met with a hurried, fearful face that stared out over the draped form of a body on a gurney.

"I hope you've had something to eat since I saw you last," Pelleter said to Madame Rosenkrantz.

She hung her head, resuming the position she no doubt had held for the last three days, her knees together, her shoulders hunched forward, her hands held in her lap, the pose of a praying supplicant. In other words, a daughter in mourning.

"Yes. The nurses feed me."

Pelleter found another chair and turned it around just inside the door. He straddled it, resting his elbows on its back. The five coffins had been piled in two stacks to the side, and there was a sour smell of decay in the enclosed room.

"Your husband has been quite distraught over your absence."

"But you knew where I was." She spoke to her hands.

"Yes."

"And you didn't tell him."

Pelleter remained silent.

"When I was a girl, I would tell people that both my parents were dead…It was easier than admitting that my father was in prison…I never saw him and I had nothing to do with him, so it was almost like he was dead, and I would forget that it wasn't true. Every now and then the thought would startle me that my father was still alive. I'd stop whatever I was doing, and think, my father is alive, but it wasn't real. In truth, I believed my own lie."

She spoke mechanically. There was none of the self-assurance, or meekness, or emotion, or any of the conflicting tempers she had shown at dinner three nights before. Her face was white, and her tone was flat.

"I didn't even tell my husband the truth until after we had moved to Verargent, and at that point I had known him for over a year. Verargent was his idea. It was small, quiet, had the train but nothing else to attract people, and so he thought it would be the ideal place to live so that he could write undisturbed. I went along with it, only half-realizing the proximity to my father. It seemed to me, what difference could it make if I was twenty miles or one hundred from him, so I didn't say anything until after we had bought our house. Even then I only explained that my father was in prison, not that he was in Malniveau."

She spoke as though the body before her wasn't the man she was speaking of.

"I told you that I believed my father had murdered my mother, and that's true, and I told you that I didn't hate him, and that's true too...

"When I was little, he taught me how to take apart his watch and put it back together. My mother told him that was for little boys, but he said he didn't care. His daughter could do anything. He set the watch on the table, and took out his tools, and he showed me piece by piece, pulling each little gear and spring out of the bronze case and spreading them out on a cloth. There were all these pieces of metal, and I couldn't understand how they could keep track of all of the seconds in the day. I thought that somehow the time must be contained in them, but when they were apart, everything went on, and when they were together, it wasn't really different. Except, I remember when the last pieces went into the watch, and he would wind it, and the second hand would start turning, it felt as though we had started the world again.

"He was so patient with me those times. And he was not always a patient man. My mother got plenty of smacks and beatings when he felt things weren't being done right…"

Pelleter reached into his inside pocket for a cigar, but he found that there were none there. He had smoked them all during the day.

"Other than that, I don't have any good memories of my father. He wasn't around a lot, and when he was, he frightened me. He could be laughing and he'd have my mother laughing, and then he'd suddenly start hitting her, or he'd storm out. I tried to stay out of his way.

"Do other people feel as though they are a part of their parents? Do they feel that the pieces of each of these grown strangers are really the parts that make them up? Can they say, this part is my mother and this part is my father? And if so, does it matter if their mother or father is still alive? If your parents die, are you the only part still living, or has a part of you died as well?"

She looked up as though she expected Pelleter to answer, and he could see just how young she was.

"I don't know," he said.

She looked at the shrouded form on the table in front of her. "I don't know either. But I don't want to be what's left of my father. He was a bad man. I know that, even if I don't feel it.

"When my mother was killed, they took me away to live with my aunt and cousins. My father was missing at that point… They found him later and then he went to prison, but I had already started telling people that both of my parents were dead…For me it was as though I was an accident created out of nothing. Maybe I was a bad person, and that was why I was all alone."

"I don't think you're a bad person," Pelleter said. "What your parents do is not your fault."

"Then why did I lie all those years?"

"That doesn't make you a bad person. And in a way, it was true."

"No," she said, shaking her head. She reached out as though she were going to touch the sheet, and then drew back, gripping the hand that she had extended in her other hand. "It wasn't true. I can tell you that now. There's absent, and there's dead, and there's a difference. Because when he was just absent, then he was still out there in the world, affecting people, causing things, even if it was only to cause the prison cook to cook one extra meal and for a guard to check his name on a piece of paper. And even if I couldn't imagine his life, and I didn't know who he was really, my idea of him seemed as though it were outside of me.

"But now that he's dead, he's nowhere but in my head. What was he to the people in the prison? Nothing. One more prisoner. He's just gone. But here…" She paused, and her eyes narrowed, the great strain of her thoughts and emotions somehow making her more precious, more delicate. She shook her head. "Now it's only building that watch, and…" She shook her head again as though shaking the thoughts away.

Pelleter could see how hurt she was, and he wanted to step around the gurney and to put a fatherly arm around her, to reassure her. But he knew it wasn't his place. He stayed seated in his chair.

"I haven't pulled back the sheet," she said. "I haven't looked at him directly…But I don't need to."

"Why don't you go home? Your husband's worried about you."

She nodded her head, but without taking her eyes off of her father's corpse. She had not cried once during her whole confession, but she looked wan and emptied.

"He loves you. He thinks you are not just a good person, but the best person. He'd do anything for you."

"I know," she said, almost a whisper.

"I'm just about finished with the case."

She looked at him then, but it didn't look as though she saw him. "It doesn't matter."

"It might not. But for the living, it's all we can ever do."

"It's still nothing. I am nineteen years old and I am finally an orphan for real. Knowing that it's going to happen, and having it happen…Not the same."

Pelleter stood at that. The smell of the dead was going to his head. He felt as though it was surrounding them, and pulling them away from the world outside. He went to her then, and helped her to her feet with a firm hand on her elbow.

As he did, there was the squeak of a rubber soled shoe on the floor in the hallway. Pelleter listened without showing that he was listening, not wanting to alarm Madame Rosenkrantz. Had he been followed again? There was no other sound and he began to guide her towards the door.

Madame Rosenkrantz didn't resist his guidance, and he led her out into the hall, where the door to the men's ward was still easing shut on its hinges, no doubt the footsteps from a moment before. But when they went into the ward, there was no one there other than the same nurse who was now removing the dinner trays from each of the patients' tables.

The nurse looked up at them with a matronly frown.

Pelleter stopped. "Did someone just come through here?"

"All you folks running through, and it's not even visiting hours. I'm going to give that girl at the front desk a talking to."

Pelleter looked ahead, and then he steered Madame Rosenkrantz back the way they had come.

The back hallway was empty still. The radio was off.

"What is it?" Madame Rosenkrantz said, awakening somewhat from her mourning stupor.

"Nothing yet."

Pelleter stood in the center of the hall, holding tight to Madame Rosenkrantz's arm and thinking. He pushed her up against the wall shared with the ward, and he went back to the morgue doorway.

He opened the door, but the room was as they had left it, storing the dead.

He returned to Madame Rosenkrantz and took her arm again, steering her down the hall as though she were luggage. She had to take small hurried steps to match his long strides, but she didn't complain and didn't ask questions.

They passed through a windowless door at the end of the hall, and found themselves in an alley beside the building.

There was a man at the end of the alley, a large silhouette peering around the side of the building watching the front entrance. He turned at the sound of them, startled to find them behind him, and then he ran out into the street, disappearing from view.

Pelleter pushed Madame Rosenkrantz back into the hospital, saying sharply, "Wait here," and he ran down the alley after the man.

The chief inspector reached the street just in time to see his quarry turn down one of the side streets that would lead him back into a series of uneven small passageways where houses had been built with no regard for keeping a thoroughfare.

The chief inspector darted after him. The blood was rushing up his arms and into his chest, constricting his airway. His heart beat dangerously in his head. He had not seen the man's face, but he had seen the man's size. He was a hulk.

The side street the man had taken was little more than an alley itself, and unlit. The crisp spring Verargent night was bright, but little of the light from the sky found its way down to these twisted cobble passages.

Pelleter plunged forward, almost twisting his ankle on one of the cobblestones, running after nothing, since there was nothing visible ahead of him.

He passed other openings, any one of which his man could have taken, and so he slowed his pace, trying to hear the other man's footsteps over his own labored breathing. Running through back alleys was a young man's work. Pelleter was no longer young.

He stopped, but heard nothing but his own body's protest.

An oval ceramic tile screwed into the side of one of the buildings read "Rue Victor Hugo." The provincialism of this almost made him laugh. To have a Rue Victor Hugo had apparently been deemed necessary, but that Verargent had settled on this back alley for the designation was small-town politics in its most essential form.

He waited another moment, straining for some sign, and then he turned back.

As he did a large form materialized out of one of the doorways and brought both hands down on the back of the chief inspector's neck, dropping Pelleter to his knees. A sharp jolt of pain shot from his kneecaps into his stomach, which threatened to empty itself.

The man swung again, still a two-fisted blow, this one landing across the chief inspector's cheek, unbalancing the downed man, who fell to the ground.

Dazed, the chief inspector tried to look up at his attacker, but there was not enough light. The man pulled back, preparing to kick Pelleter in the ribs, and the chief inspector instinctively put his arms around his head, pulling his body into a ball.

The blow did not come.

Footsteps echoed and were soon beyond hearing.

The chief inspector rolled onto his back, looking up at the lighter patch of sky between the buildings. He took deep breaths, trying to control his breathing, to steady his heart rate.

He looked at his surroundings to distract himself from the pain. All of the windows were shuttered for the night. No one had seen the attack. The ceramic street marker caught a glint of light from somewhere, winking at Pelleter on the ground. Wink, wink. Wink, wink.

It was not the first time he had been beaten, but it had been a long time, many years, and he had forgotten what kinds of little details got imprinted on the mind in such moments. The winking Rue Victor Hugo! There was one in every town!

When his body had recovered enough to let him feel the throbbing ache stemming from the top of his spine, and the sharp pain radiating from his cheekbone, Pelleter pulled himself up to a standing position, leaning one hand against the wall beside him.

His body had to accommodate the pain to his upright position, sending a shiver over Pelleter's frame. He was thankful that his attacker held off that final kick. The man could have gotten away without any confrontation. But a panicked man too often made bad decisions. Once he struck he must have come to his senses.

Who had Pelleter angered? Or maybe the right question was, who had he scared? The lineup at the prison had clearly worried someone, if he was being followed and attacked. But too many of the guards could be described as large men for Pelleter's shadowy impression of his assailant to be any help at identification. Pelleter had thought he was close, at least to identifying the people who knew most of the answers, but there must be some piece that he was missing.

He took his hand away from the wall, testing his weight on his feet, and rolled his head to one side, wincing with the movement. He started back the way he had come, towards the hospital.

°

The nurse behind the front desk stood as he came in. Half of the lights in the building had been doused, creating the cavernous feel of a public institution at night.

"I'll get the resident physician," she said, her weight already shifting, ready.

"No," the chief inspector said. "I'm fine."

Madame Rosenkrantz was sitting in one of the chairs along the wall of the main entry hall, her lost blank expression back on her face. She looked up at Pelleter as he came in, but she made no comment about the bruise he could already feel welling up on his face. When he held out his hand, she stood up, and walked past him out the front entrance.

The nurse, still standing, watched them go, shaking her head, but whether in disapproval or disbelief, it could not be said.

Outside, Madame Rosenkrantz did not speak, nor did she ask where they were going. He took her by the arm and led her back to the center of town where a single car was crossing the square, and then out to the Rosenkrantz home.

In front of the gate to her house, she stopped, resisting, and he at last let go of her elbow.

She looked at him, and there was some color in her cheeks from the walk. Her eyes seemed more focused, but the pain was still written across her face. "Will this ever stop?" she said.

"You should be safe now," he said.

She shook her head. That was not what she had meant.

He nodded. "It'll stop." But his neck ached, and he did not know.

"I guess I thought he'd always be there for me if I really needed him."

"Have you needed him?" Pelleter said.

"No."

"Go home to your husband."

She put her hand on the gate, and Pelleter turned away, heading back into town without watching whether or not she really went home. When he was a few steps away, he heard the gate close behind him.

He ate dinner alone at the hotel, and he called his wife before going to bed just to say good night.

In the morning, Pelleter was in high spirits, even with the soreness from the previous night's adventure. When he had come to Verargent, it had been to receive the testimony of an already incarcerated prisoner, no more than a day trip. Five days later, there were six dead bodies—seven, if he was not mistaken—at least one other murder attempt, and a building full of suspects. But today, Sunday, he was certain that he would have the answers to his questions, and that he could go home.

In the hotel lobby, he found Officer Martin sleeping in the lion's-footed armchair Fournier had waited in Friday night. Martin was dressed in the same uniform he had worn yesterday, now thoroughly wrinkled, and a day's growth of beard covered his face. He had a number of files clutched to his chest, his arms crossed over them.

Pelleter called to the boy behind the counter, somebody he had never seen before, "How long has he been here?"

"I come on at seven and he was here then."

It was only a little before eight now. The first train from the city came into Verargent at nine-forty, and Pelleter wanted to be there when Lambert arrived with his prisoner.

He hated to wake Martin if the man had been working most of the night, but there was nothing to be done about it. Besides, Letreau wouldn't want one of his men to be seen with his mouth hanging open in the hotel lobby. He reached out and touched the young man's shoulder.

Martin started, grimaced, and looked around without moving his head, a quizzical expression on his face. "Inspector," he said, stretching in the seat, and then sitting upright, letting his burden of files down into his lap. He rubbed a hand across his face, and then became aware of the fact that he was being observed by a superior officer. His eyes went wide, and he prepared to stand.

"Inspector, I'm sorry, I must have fallen asleep. I wanted to be sure to get you these."

He started to sort through the files on his lap.

"It's okay," Pelleter said, amused at the young man's enthusiasm. It seemed to contribute to the upbeat temper at the end of a case. "Take your time. No need to stand. What time did you get in?"

"Maybe five. What time is it now?"

"Eight."

Martin had the files in order now, and he looked up at the chief inspector. His eyes went wide for a second time at the sight of Pelleter's battered face. "What happened?"

"Apparently somebody thinks we're too close to finished. Once you show me those files, I have a feeling we might know who."

Martin handed three of them up to Pelleter. They were thick files with years of paperwork on uneven paper of various colors, the oldest sheets an almost amber-brown.

Pelleter opened the first one. It was Passemier's, the guard who had had nothing to say. He had been a large man. It was possible that he had been Pelleter's attacker, but he had seemed too certain of his invincibility. "Fournier let you take these out of the prison?"

Martin went slightly red. "Fournier wasn't there, and I thought nobody would mind…"

Pelleter opened the second file, which was the warden's. It showed that his service had begun in 1899, the same as Passemier, on cell block D. While Pelleter looked, Martin talked:

"You were right, as you can see. Those three men all started as guards at Malniveau within a few years of one another."

The third file was for a man named Soldaux. He had started in 1896, also on cell block D. The top of his file had been stamped, "Retired."

"And if you look at their detail…"

"All three worked the same cell block when they started. Does Soldaux still live in town?"

"Yes."

Pelleter smiled and nodded, looking off into the distance. It looked as though he might burst out singing. He would not be surprised at all to find that Soldaux was also a very large man.

Martin was startled to see the inspector so pleased. He stood then, and handed the inspector the file in his hand, coming around so that he could look at it at the same time as Pelleter.

"If you look here…Since the files of the murdered prisoners were marked transferred, I got the idea that we should see what a file looked like if a prisoner was murdered and it was marked properly…"

This was another old file, as full as the others. It was for a prisoner named Renaud Leclerc. He had been sent to Malniveau in 1894 on a conspiracy charge, an anarchist believed responsible for a series of bombings in which several people were injured although no one was killed.

Martin, excited over his discovery, talked faster than Pelleter could read. "Leclerc was killed two months ago, at least a month before any of the men found in the field. He had no family any longer, so he was buried here in Verargent, which is why we didn't know about it. The police are only informed if the body has to go out by train."

"Good work, my boy," Pelleter said, still reading through Leclerc's history. "Good work."

Martin beamed, and his broad smile juxtaposed with his shabby appearance was comic. He had the makings of a fine detective.

Pelleter closed the file, and looked closely into Martin's face. "Listen to me, we're nearly finished. This is what I need you to do…Go to Soldaux's house, and bring him to

Town Hall. Stop by the station and get a partner first. He may not want to come with you, and I don't want him getting away...I have a feeling he'll be a big man...yes, I'm certain of it...Then the same with Passemier. Again, two men...I have to meet the nine-forty train with Chief Letreau...Do you think you can handle this?"

"Yes."

"Don't take any unnecessary risks."

Martin waited expectantly for the inspector to say something else, but Pelleter continued to look off into the distance with a smile on his lips.

"Yes..." the inspector said to himself. His smile broadened. He saw that Martin was still standing next to him. "Go. Go. I want everybody there by ten-thirty at the latest."

Martin turned and practically ran out the door. Pelleter wasn't far behind.

The weather fit the inspector's mood, not a trace of the storm from earlier in the week. It looked as though it never rained in Verargent.

"Inspector," somebody called as Pelleter turned towards the police station. Officer Martin was already out of sight. "Inspector!"

It was Servières.

Pelleter didn't stop, but instead called behind him, "Come to the station around ten o'clock. You'll get your story then."

Servières surprised at this jovial command, stopped short, and Pelleter hurried on to the police station.

°

The Verargent train station was little more than a wide
patch of beaten dirt at the side of the track just outside of
town. A small wooden enclosure open on two sides had
been built at some time to offer protection from the ele-
ments, but it had clearly long been a target of vandalism
for the Verargent youth. There was a hole through the
roof, and every square inch had been carved into more
than once.

Pelleter and Letreau stood under the post that read
*Verargent* outside of the enclosure. The weather was
warm, and Pelleter had removed his jacket and held it
draped over his arm. He whistled as he looked down the
length of railroad track that cut through the countryside.

Letreau paced, impatient. He appeared less ragged
than the day before, but still on edge.

"I hope you know what you're doing," he said, not for
the first time. He had already asked Pelleter about his
injuries and had not been happy that the chief inspector
had not given him much of an answer.

"We'll know soon enough," Pelleter said, and resumed
whistling.

"It's all well and good for you, but I have to live here.
We don't want any problems with the prison. We want to
forget that it's there. I haven't spent so much time out
there in one week in my life."

The distant steam of the locomotive could be seen on
the horizon.

"I hope you know what you're doing."

Now that the train was visible, Letreau stopped, and
stood beside Pelleter. Pelleter put his jacket back on,
and put his hands in his pockets. He would have liked to

smoke a cigar, but he had not had a chance to replenish his supply.

"You hope to leave tonight?" Letreau said.

"That's the plan."

"It'll really be tied up?"

"You might not have all the answers you want, but I think you'll have the ones you need."

"My wife'll never forgive you for skipping all those dinners."

The tracks began to sing their metallic whine.

The two policemen stood side by side like immovable objects. The train whistle sounded, and the air brakes hissed while the train was still two hundred yards away. The chuff chuff of the wheels slowed, the expanse of metal slowing impossibly, and then the engine stopped just past them, and the escaping hiss of gas marked the train's arrival in Verargent.

A round-hatted conductor appeared on the platform of the first car before them, and called, "Verargent," and then Lambert appeared.

Pelleter smiled at the sight of his old friend and colleague, but he didn't take his hands out of his pockets.

"You are some trouble, aren't you?" Lambert called, as he stepped down.

Behind him, a tight, pale face appeared, an older man carrying two large leather cases in front of him.

"I hope you know what you're doing," Letreau said again, a refrain that had long since lost its meaning.

The older man stepped down as well. The warden of Malniveau Prison was home.

# 13.

## Thirty-two Years

Being escorted home by a national police inspector had made the warden quiet. He looked as though he were in danger of throwing up at any moment.

His wife, however, had no qualms about laying into Inspector Pelleter.

"Who do you think you are that you have us taken on a train against our will, and on our vacation, too! My husband is a very important man. You think you can push him around!"

The warden ignored his wife's outburst, and headed directly for the police car that was parked just off the side of the road near the train stop.

Letreau tried to catch Pelleter's eye, but unable to, he turned to follow the warden.

"The reason we have an assistant warden is just so that this kind of thing does not happen," the warden's wife continued, her cloying perfume sweetening the air. "It's not a one-man job, certainly not anymore, now that my husband's not a young man. You take this up with Fournier. We would have been back tomorrow."

"I'm sorry to have cut your vacation short, madame," Pelleter said, and he smiled at Lambert behind her back.

The warden's wife went to the police car and got in back with her husband.

"Did you have any trouble?" Pelleter asked Lambert.

"We were getting that speech from both of them at first, but when I insisted, he got really quiet. He's been like that since."

"Sorry to bring you out here like this. We'll go back together tonight."

"That's no problem. After a day with those two, I'm curious to see where this is all going."

Pelleter opened the passenger door of the police car. The warden's wife was still complaining. "So am I," he said, and got into the car.

The scene at the Verargent police station was amusing to Pelleter's practiced eye for its studied busyness. Every desk was occupied by an officer diligent about his paperwork, and an additional officer stood near one of the walls with a case file open much as a man reads a newspaper while waiting for the bus. Word must have spread that Inspector Pelleter was bringing in the chief suspects. All eyes darted up at their entrance.

"Monsieur Letreau, you tell me what's going on. No one is talking to me. And I keep telling them, if they would just get in touch with Monsieur Fournier, he will take care of any problem at the prison. These city people treat us like we can be pushed around…"

It was the warden's wife, still voicing her complaints with no regard for who was around her.

"Marie!" the warden snapped, the first he had spoken since arriving on the train. He grabbed his wife by the arm and pulled her to him, whispering fiercely into her ear.

She screwed up her face, tightening the muscles of her

arm and pulling away from him, but without any serious attempt to break free.

Philippe Servières was in a corner writing excitedly in his open notebook. He caught Pelleter's eye, nodded, and smiled, holding up the notebook in thanks. Pelleter did not acknowledge the reporter.

"Has Martin returned with his prisoners?" Pelleter asked the man at the front desk.

The officer stammered and looked away as though to hide the fact that he had been paying attention to the new arrivals, "I, um, no, Martin? Martin's out with Arnaud, sir."

"Let me know when he arrives." Pelleter turned to Letreau. "Your office?"

"That's fine."

Pelleter nodded, flicking his eyes to Lambert, and then the warden. "*Monsieur le Directeur*."

Lambert stepped in to separate the warden and his wife, and the warden's wife began to complain again at once, her voice carrying despite her attempt at restraint. "No, this will not do." Lambert tried to take her arm, but she pulled it away, and stood her ground. "This is not acceptable."

Ignoring the woman's protestations, Letreau, Pelleter, and the warden went into Letreau's office where Pelleter offered the warden a chair as Letreau closed the door on the now buzzing squad room.

Pelleter had arranged the files that Officer Martin had borrowed from Malniveau Prison into a pile on the corner of the desk closest to the warden. They formed an uneven sheaf of papers as thick as a phone book.

Pelleter leaned back against the desk, reaching into

his pocket for a cigar, but he still had not replenished his supply. He was eager for a smoke.

The warden's eyes darted to the files and then to Pelleter.

Pelleter crossed his arms. "Do you know what these are?" he said, indicating the stack with a nod of his head.

Letreau made a noise as he positioned himself against the closed door, and the warden looked behind him, having to raise himself against the arms of the chair in order to do so. He turned back with an exhalation, and shook his head.

Pelleter smirked despite himself. "Do you have a guess?"

"Should I have my lawyer present?" The warden spoke with the restraint of a powerful man uncertain if his power was a handicap in the situation.

"I think we're all interested in keeping this simple," Pelleter said, glancing over the top of the warden's head at Letreau as though they were all coming to an agreement. "We'll just try to keep to the truth, and be quick about it, and it shouldn't be a problem."

The warden sat with his lips pressed together.

"These files," Pelleter said, tenting his fingers on top of them, "are your records and the records of guards Passemier and Soldaux and of a prisoner named Renaud Leclerc."

The warden's shoulders slumped, his whole body adopting the aspect of a man too tired even to sit.

"Could you tell us about the prisoner Renaud Leclerc?"

"Oh—" The warden's voice broke, and he cleared his throat, coughed, and adjusted himself in the seat with the assistance of the armrests again. "Well, I'd have to look in his file and…"

"I would have thought that you would have been familiar with the case of the last prisoner to be murdered under your watch. Perhaps we should contact Monsieur Fournier as your wife said…"

The warden sighed, and looked back at Letreau who was impassive. He faced forward, adjusting himself in the chair again. "Leclerc was an anarchist back when the anarchists were dropping bombs everywhere…He was involved in a bombing and was caught, and he was sent here. This must have been in the early '90s. But then some years later he killed a fellow prisoner here, and his sentence was extended. After that, he was a model prisoner until he was killed himself two months ago."

"Why would anyone want to kill Leclerc?"

"I don't know."

"But he was the first of this series of killings?"

The warden didn't answer.

"In your opinion, *Monsieur le Directeur*, did Leclerc kill that other prisoner? Think before you answer!" Pelleter added.

The warden opened his mouth. He looked again at Letreau and then back at the stack of files on the edge of the chief of police's desk.

Pelleter jumped on this. "Are you wondering how much the files say? Are you worried you might tell us more than we know? What could we possibly know other than that Soldaux and Passemier were also guards on cell block D in 1899? Leclerc's file must certainly show that he really killed the prisoner he was accused of killing."

"Did you say there had been other stabbings?" the warden said, trying on his authority again to see if he still had it. "What does this have to do with that, such an old business?"

He appealed to the silent Letreau again, for there was no one else to appeal to, and this time the chief of police's face did seem to carry the same question.

Pelleter ignored this, leaning in until his face was only inches from the warden's. "What you should really be asking yourself is, how much have Soldaux and Passemier already told us?"

Pelleter sat back and recrossed his arms.

The warden looked around the room, and then back at Pelleter.

"I should have a lawyer here," the warden said, his eyes pleading.

Pelleter didn't soften. Neither of the lawmen spoke.

The warden brought his right palm to his hairline, kneading his temples, and then slid his hand to the back of his head. He looked away from either of the other two men. "It was thirty-two years ago…" he began. "I had just started at Malniveau. I was young and a bit of a brute. There are only so many ways to get into trouble in Verargent without going too far…I had finished school, and I knew I was too old to keep getting into little fights, but I didn't know what else to do. So I started working in the prison. I liked the idea of being in charge…Passemier started with me at the same time. We hadn't been friends in school, but we ran in the same circles…Soldaux was the senior guard on the duty, although he was only a few years older…He was like a big brother to us."

The warden shrugged and shook his head, smiling ironically at the memory.

"Back then, you could do more to the prisoners and get away with it. Sometimes on night duty, if we were really bored, we'd give one of the prisoners…a hard time."

He checked to see if Pelleter had understood. The chief inspector's expression was easy, but his eyes were locked on the warden, and it made the warden look away again. The hand went again to the back of his head.

"One night we went too far and the prisoner died…I wasn't in the room when it happened, naturally…I don't know which of Soldaux or Passemier struck the fatal blow…"

"Naturally," Pelleter said, straining to keep his voice level.

"We were kids really, and we were just fooling around, but this guy was weak, and he didn't make it…"

"Jesus," Letreau said, behind the warden.

"We panicked. We didn't want to end up as prisoners ourselves. The man had clearly been beaten, so we couldn't claim that he had died of natural causes…So we fell on the man's cellmate, Leclerc…We gave him a light beating, just enough to land him in the infirmary, in order to make it appear as though the two men had fought. When Leclerc came around the next day, he learned that he'd already taken the fall for the murder. We let him know we would look out for him, and make sure that nobody bothered him."

"Which was better for him than him having an 'accident' if he ever claimed a different story."

The warden said nothing.

"Well, somebody got to him in the end."

The warden shrugged and looked down. "In the end. I'm warden now, so I'm rarely on the cell block myself. Soldaux had retired. Passemier was on a different duty. We couldn't protect him always."

"And he couldn't go anywhere."

Letreau cleared his throat. "Inspector, this is revelatory, but what does it have to do with anything?" The chief of police needed *his* murder solved, not just any murder.

Pelleter held up a staying hand to quiet Letreau. He prompted the warden. "So when Leclerc was murdered..."

"It was a shock."

"But at the same time a relief, no? You were off the hook. Finally."

The warden didn't respond, and Letreau shifted, impatient. The buzz from the squad room had grown enough to penetrate the office door, a quiet roar from the room outside.

Pelleter said, "But then another prisoner was killed..."

"It's one thing for one prisoner to die in a stabbing," the warden said, almost annoyed. "That happens. But a second one...it would have raised questions. Maybe even reopened the first case. I couldn't risk my position as warden."

"Especially when you and Passemier are only three years away from retirement yourselves." Pelleter looked up at Letreau and he saw that the chief of police got it, or at least this part of it. Pelleter didn't want the warden to stop talking now that he was so unrestrained. The chief inspector pushed him again: "They had already sent

Fournier to look after you. You hoped that he would just be your successor when you retired, but you couldn't know for sure he wasn't there to replace you…"

"It wasn't just me. Passemier was even more worried—and Soldaux, for his pension. I told them, it's been three decades, there's no way the old incident would come to light now, and yet…Unnecessary questions might just uncover unnecessary answers about Leclerc's past…Soldaux built the coffin, and we used his truck. We're not young men anymore, but we were able to rise to the challenge."

"So when the third prisoner was killed, and the fourth…"

"That's right. We just kept on."

"How many in all?"

"After Leclerc? Five, plus Meranger. Six, then."

"What if the prisoners' families came looking for them?"

"Some had no family, or none who cared to stay in contact. For those that did…We'd record the prisoners as having been transferred…The ensuing investigation would either give us time to get out of the country, or come up with an alternate explanation."

"And the prison is large enough that you were able to keep the number of stabbings, and how many of them had ended in deaths, a secret…"

"People might know some things, but no one would know everything."

"But what about Meranger," burst out Letreau, not happy with how long Pelleter was taking to get there.

Pelleter reached for a cigar again, and then remembered that he didn't have any before his hand even went inside his jacket. "The night Meranger was killed it was raining. It was raining much too heavily to bury a body in a field. So they had to get rid of it another way. Am I right?"

"Yes," the warden said.

"They changed Meranger into civilian clothes and dumped him in town, figuring that it would be assumed he had escaped, and then been killed by his accomplices after the fact."

Letreau shook his head, and said, "The things people do."

"Of course, the same downpour that prevented them from burying Meranger uncovered the hastily buried coffins of the other prisoners."

The warden just shook his head in disbelief. "Thirty-two years…" he said.

The pitch of the noise from the squad room changed, and Letreau stepped away from the door, a puzzled expression on his face.

Pelleter stood. When Letreau looked back, the inspector nodded that the chief of police should open the door.

Everyone was on their feet in the station. Martin, Arnaud, and Lambert were wrestling a large man in his sixties around the booking desk. His arms were pulled back, his hands cuffed behind his back. In the background, a stunned Rosenkrantz, his arm protectively enveloping his wife, floated near the front door.

The warden stood, and Pelleter put a hand on his upper arm, although he was not concerned that the warden was about to run.

Letreau stepped up to where the struggle was going on as the prisoner kicked one of the desks several inches, and then Lambert tripped the man so that he came down onto the desk face first, dragging Martin and Arnaud with him, who held on.

Pelleter was pleased to see that he had been right. The man was six-four, easily two hundred fifty pounds, and looked like a powerhouse despite his gray hair.

Pelleter led the warden out of Letreau's office, and as soon as the downed man saw the warden, he shouted, "You bastard!" Lambert knew to step forward and relieve Pelleter of the warden. "You ran out on us!" Soldaux shouted at the warden.

"Monsieur Soldaux, thank you for joining us," the chief inspector said. "It's so nice to see you again, and really get a good look at you."

The large man struggled on the desk, wriggling his shoulders. "I've never seen you before in my life, and I wish I never did."

Pelleter brought his hand up to his bruised cheek, reassuring himself with the tender throb that was there under pressure. He looked over the prisoner, thinking. The warden's wife stood, so stunned that she was speechless. Servières was writing it all down.

"Where's Passemier?" Pelleter said suddenly.

"He wasn't home."

Pelleter turned to the warden. "Does he have a car?"

"No."

Letreau stepped forward, reasserting his command. "Put these men in the holding cell. Everyone else must have something to do. So start doing it."

The stunned atmosphere began to retake its normal shape. Letreau trailed his prisoners further into Town Hall.

Lambert joined Pelleter, who had not moved since asking about Passemier.

"We need to find the other guard. He attacked me last night."

"I'd wondered what happened to your face. I figured you'd fallen while shaving."

Pelleter gave that as much of a smile as it deserved. There was yelling from the back corridor now, and the warden's wife was arguing with two of the other officers, asking where her husband had been taken.

"Inspector." It was Rosenkrantz.

Pelleter raised an index finger to hold him off and continued talking to Lambert. "See if you can get Letreau. Tell him we need to start a stakeout. The train station, all of the major roads out of town. If Passemier's still here, we don't want him to get away."

Lambert began to go, but stopped when the chief inspector spoke again.

"And we'll need a warrant. I want to search the man's house."

"Inspector, I wanted to thank…"

Pelleter let his raised hand drop. Rosenkrantz had stepped up to the booking desk. He held Clotilde so close that she had to stand at an angle to walk. Her hand lay flat on her husband's chest.

"Inspector…you were as good as your word, and I want you to know I'm grateful. For everything you did."

The words seemed to carry an extra weight, as though

he meant to thank Pelleter for more than just his wife's return. Had he told Clotilde of his binge the other night? Probably not.

"No need to thank me," Pelleter said. "Anyway, it's not over yet."

# 14.

## *Roadblock*

In Verargent, searching for missing children could be done on anyone's authority. Arranging the complicated machinations involved in tracking down a fugitive—the necessary roadblocks, the search warrant for his home, informing the railroad—required the approval of the town magistrate.

The portion of Town Hall used for the administrative operations of the town distinguished itself from the police station with high ceilings. The light fixtures hung on long cords overhead, casting self-important shadows.

Pelleter paced in the hall outside the magistrate's office. Letreau was inside. Pelleter imagined he was taking great care to show that all actions had been taken under his authority, embarrassed now at how flustered he had been in the preceding few days. In the meantime, he had had the sense to set up the roadblocks first and to get the paperwork done afterwards.

Pelleter cast an impatient glance at the closed office door with each pass. The bruise on his face seemed alive with worry, three pinpricks of red in the center of the wound. He had sent Lambert to the train station in anticipation of the midday train to the city. Servières had gone with Lambert, certain that the story was with him.

Pelleter stopped in front of the magistrate's door,

willing it to open. Letreau's officers were in the process
of cutting off the main routes of escape, but something
worried him. It was not that they might be too late. If
Passemier had been planning to run the night before,
then following and attacking Pelleter would have been
counter to his plans. It was the attack itself that bothered
him. People made rash decisions when they felt cornered.
Passemier was violent and a murderer and he had already
shown what something as simple as an informal interrogation would drive him to. If they cut off his escape routes,
what would be his next move?

Pelleter touched the bruise on his cheek and rolled his
shoulders, satisfying himself that the pain was unchanged.
Madame Pelleter would have scolded him for playing
with his wounds.

The door to the magistrate's office opened and Letreau
emerged holding up a sheaf of papers. "Let's go," he said.

Pelleter caught a glimpse through the door behind the
chief of police, but it opened only onto an outer office
where a secretary sat at a desk. The town magistrate was
hidden away in some interior office, doubly protected
from the town he administered.

The two men headed towards the connecting hall that
led back to the police station.

"Where are we going?" Pelleter said.

The chief inspector was not surprised when Letreau
answered, "Rue Victor Hugo."

In daylight, the Rue Victor Hugo showed itself to be little
more than an alley, similar to the one where Rosenkrantz
had gotten drunk in the basement pub. At some time after

the alley had formed between the surrounding buildings, an attempt had been made for drainage by lining the center of the cobblestone path with a concave well of brick. The project had been ill conceived, however, since puddles lined the edges of the alley even five days after the rain. Pelleter saw that he had been lucky not to break an ankle on his chase the night before.

The concierge for Passemier's building lived two buildings away on the corner of Rue Victor Hugo and another alley that had not been deemed worthy of a name. She was a worn, middle-aged woman doing the washing outside her door in a large tin tub with a washboard.

"Have you been up there yet?" she asked, not stopping her washing.

"An officer was there earlier, and no one answered," Letreau explained. "You see we have the warrant. We just need you to let us in."

She was unconvinced. "I don't know anything about a warrant. I've been concierge of this building, that one, and that other one," she pointed with her chin, "for seven years now, and I've never seen anything about a warrant. Monsieur Passemier works out at the prison as a guard."

Letreau blew out his cheeks, and then opened his mouth to speak, but Pelleter stepped forward. "Madame, I appreciate your caution. If all concierges were as cautious as you, then perhaps the police wouldn't have as much work as we do."

The woman narrowed her eyes, unsure if he was truly complimenting her or mocking her.

Pelleter wondered how close this spot was to where he had been beaten the night before. The concierge might have been one of the many nonexistent witnesses. "We don't think that Monsieur Passemier is home or that there is any trouble in your building. But we need to ask Monsieur Passemier a few questions, and we were hoping that something in his apartment would tell us where he had gone."

The concierge regarded Pelleter for another moment, pausing in her scrubbing and blowing a stray strand of hair out of her eyes. She looked at Letreau. "That paper means I don't have a choice, does it?"

Pelleter tried a kind smile and nodded an apology.

She began scrubbing again and nodded with her head towards the open door behind her. "All the keys are on the ring just inside the door. It's got the number on it."

Letreau went forward to find the keys, and Pelleter said, "Thank you."

They waited awkwardly a moment while the woman continued washing, before Letreau came back with a key ring.

The two lawmen went partway down the alley, further from the main street that led to the hospital. The concierge watched them.

When they got to the door, which was a few steps below street level, they found it partially ajar.

"Guess we didn't need the key after all," Pelleter said.

"Damn it," Letreau said. He looked at Pelleter. "What do we do?"

Martin had not said that the door had been opened, so either Passemier had been home when the officer had knocked and had since left, had come and gone in the meantime and forgotten to close the door, or the prison guard was home now and didn't expect to be there long.

Pelleter pulled out his revolver, and, taking a deep breath, Letreau did the same. Then Pelleter pushed his way in.

"Hello!" Letreau called.

The apartment had the mustiness of a below-ground room. Pelleter wondered if it flooded when it rained, like the baker's basement.

"I guess you don't make much as a prison guard," Letreau said, looking around.

"Or he didn't have much reason to spend money on anything," Pelleter said.

The flat was furnished with the barest of necessities, a few chairs, a table, a single shelf with assorted books. Everything was neat, because there was nothing to make it cluttered.

A hall opened off to the right at the back of the room, and there was an opening to the left. Pelleter nodded to the left at Letreau. Letreau turned for the opening, and Pelleter went towards the right.

The hall led to two small rooms, one that opened immediately to the right off of the hall and the other that opened straight ahead. The room to the right was a storage area. The man had accumulated some things over his lifetime, but whatever they were he had boxed away and stacked in this small space. Pelleter opened one of the boxes nearest to him and found that it was filled with newspapers. Another one had dime novels.

The room straight ahead was the bedroom. It was as spare as the others, but a chest of drawers had been emptied, the drawers left open. The bed cover had been thrown back from the bottom as though Passemier had retrieved something from below the bed. That would have been his suitcase. The night before he had planned to fight, but something had changed, and he was now clearly on the run. Had Soldaux been able to tip him off? Maybe it had just been his intuition.

Pelleter went back out into the living room and found Letreau holding a gray cat with a white speck off-center above its nose. "Look who I found enjoying a saucer of milk in the kitchen."

Pelleter stepped over to the kitchen and glanced in. It was only large enough for a stove and an icebox. A layer of grime coated everything. A single skillet hung from a nail on the wall, and the saucer of milk was on the floor. It was still mostly full. Passemier must have left only moments before. That was why the door was open. If he wasn't coming back, then the cat needed a way to get out.

"The warden said that Passemier didn't have a car," Pelleter said, back in the living room. "How would he have gotten to work?"

"Many of the guards share a ride."

"So we need to get a list of which guards have cars, and start checking them. He's definitely running for it." They had to keep moving. He took out his notebook, wrote something there, and tore off the sheet. Then he went for the door. "Come on."

Once outside, he put the note between the door and the jamb, closing the door and locking it. In the distance, the faint sound of the midday train's whistle sounded. The two men shared a look, but said nothing.

They stopped back at the concierge's where the woman was still at her washing. There were a few more articles of clothing on a line overhead, but otherwise no time might have passed.

"Here are the keys and a friend," Letreau said, taking both into her apartment.

"What are you doing with that? I can't have a cat in there!"

"Did you see Passemier in the past half-hour?" Pelleter asked.

"No. I thought you said he wasn't home."

"Let the police know if he comes back. He'll know you have his cat, we left a note."

"Is he dangerous?" the concierge said, for the first time showing real concern now that she had been given a responsibility.

The two men turned without answering.

"What am I supposed to do with the cat if he doesn't come back?"

Letreau had given his men orders to report in every hour. When he and Pelleter returned to the police station they found that nothing had changed. Lambert had also reported. The midday train had passed without incident. Letreau went to find out from the warden which of the guards had cars, and who Passemier was most likely to trust.

Pelleter sat in one of the waiting-room chairs, pulling on his lips, and occasionally putting his fingertips to the bruise on his cheek. All eyes in the police station were on

him, but he ignored the attention. He was bothered by a
sense that they were on the wrong track, that Passemier,
while brutal, was not stupid, and that he would know not
to trust any of the other prison guards. After all, while the
lines were perhaps hard to see at times, in the end, the
prison guards were on the side of the law, not crime.

The chief inspector bowed his head. He thought of
the saucer of milk laid out for the cat. Passemier was not
a sentimental man—the meager furnishings in his apartment indicated that—but he was a responsible man. Perhaps that was why he had stayed to the last minute, out of
an obligation to see the whole thing through.

And that saucer of milk had still been full. The man
was still close. They could not afford to search a list of
people. They needed to know where he was going, and
be certain of it.

Pelleter rolled his shoulders, the bruise on the top of
his spine turning white hot for a moment, and he winced.
The Verargent gendarmes continued to watch. He imagined them thinking, This is a real policeman. Injured in
the line of duty and still going on. But what was the alter-
native?

Pelleter looked back towards the hall leading to the
holding cell. Where was Letreau?

Pelleter reviewed the precautions they had taken, roadblocks and the train station. The Perreaux boys had been
found in the middle of a field. Why wouldn't Passemier
just walk around the roadblocks that way and try to catch
a ride further on down the road?

Letreau arrived with the list. "There are only ten of
them, and two are at the prison now. I just called."

"Good," Pelleter said. "Put some men on it. Then get the word out. We need to organize a search, like you did for the children, and we need to do it now."

Letreau puffed out his cheeks, "Right."

"He was still in town within the hour."

Letreau looked disconsolately at the list of names in his hand. Then he turned and shouted, "Arnaud!" and headed back to his men.

Phone calls were made. Pairs of police officers left the station. Soon there were men filing in from outside. These would be the search party. Having seen the search party from the other night, Pelleter noted that this was a different sort altogether, only young men, some who were still almost boys, all with mean faces. Several of them carried rifles. At least one of them had a pistol in a shoulder holster. They laughed and smoked, filling the public space of the station. There was none of the worried urgency of the other night. This was the excited anticipation before a football match between rivals.

Pelleter thought of the warden's description of his youth as a Verargent troublemaker.

Reports came back negative. They were losing time.

Letreau interrogated the warden and Soldaux again to see if there were any places that Passemier visited regularly, but the man led a simple life of work and then home, work and then home…and of course disposing of murdered corpses.

At last Letreau appeared with a large map of Verargent and spread it out over the front desk. "Quiet now," he yelled over the noise of the crowd.

Pelleter worked his way beside the chief of police.

"Quiet, please."

The remainder of the police force that was not currently on a roadblock or checking on other prison guards
stood in silence behind their chief.

"Gentlemen!"

"Right, now!" Pelleter said, at a stern but normal level.

The men closest to him fell silent, elbowing those
behind them. There was a last stray laugh, somebody
said, "And she will," and then, "Shut up, blockhead," and
there was quiet. The smoke from their cigarettes clouded
above them.

Letreau cleared his throat.

"Thank you all for coming." The chief of police glanced
at Pelleter for support, but the chief inspector remained
impassive. "Right. We are looking for a man by the name
of Passemier. He is six foot one, two hundred twenty-five
pounds, fifty-one years of age, with dark hair graying at
the temples. You are to assume he is armed and dangerous. We know that he was in the Rue Victor Hugo
within the last two hours and that he is most likely trying
to leave town."

Letreau held up the map and pointed.

"This is Passemier's home. We're going to conduct a
house-by-house, block-by-block search from there to the
edge of town, and we'll search through the night if we
have to. If he's still in town, that will force him to show
himself at some point."

"What, we can just go in people's houses?" one of the
men said near the front.

"There will be officers with you. You have to explain

the situation. If somebody refuses, get an officer, and he'll take care of it."

There was an uneasy pause. The men shifted on their feet.

"Any other questions?"

No one spoke.

Letreau turned to his officers. "Men, divide up the search party, and get started. I want constant updates here."

The noise started then, as the door opened, letting in a breeze and a shaft of bright light over the heads of the search party. The crowd filed through the door.

Letreau turned to Pelleter. "Do you think we'll get him?"

"Maybe not today. But we'll get him eventually."

Letreau rolled the map in front of him with both hands. "That's what I think," he said, the hint of a pleased smile on his face. "But the warden…and the other one…" He nodded to himself. "Surely you won't refuse dinner tonight!"

The crowd at the door had shrunk to just police, and then the last of those were out the door.

"Madame Pelleter will expect me back," the chief inspector said, but even as he said it, he was thinking that there was something that he was missing about Passemier's whereabouts that was important. He wanted to at least see the search through. He wouldn't feel settled if he didn't.

"And what of Madame Letreau?" Letreau said, clapping the chief inspector on the shoulder.

The Verargent chief of police was clearly feeling pleased. He had had perhaps the worst week of his career with six murdered persons showing up and two lost children. But he had suspects in custody for the bodies—even if they were not the murderers, they were responsible—and the children had been found unharmed.

"Let's see how this afternoon goes," Pelleter said.

"Right," Letreau said. "I'll tell her you're coming." And he walked back towards his office.

The police station appeared emptier for the disarray in which it had been left. The desks were scattered with papers, files left opened, fountain pens across their pages. Chairs were pushed back, and a file cabinet drawer had not been shut. The cloud of smoke from the search party's cigarettes drifted, a diffuse haze over the empty scene.

A lone officer had been left to man the phones. He was busy taking notes, the receiver of a phone cradled between his shoulder and his ear.

Here it was again. The waiting. That was perhaps all that was left with this one. It was best to be moving.

Pelleter turned to go outside. He badly needed a cigar. There was a tobacco shop in a little out-of-the-way street just off of the square. He left the station.

The weather was almost too perfect, but the chief inspector did not notice that as he crossed the square. He pictured Passemier sitting across from him in the interrogation room in the prison, first bluster, then confusion, then arrogance. Was he going through those stages again now? He had followed Pelleter two nights in a row. He had attacked him the second night. Now he was on the run. Was he confused or was he arrogant?

The chief inspector nodded to the old men around the war memorial, touching the brim of his hat. He shook his head as though he had been asked a question, and then passed on.

The warm comforting smell of tobacco enveloped him in the tobacconist's shop. Distracted, he bought three cheap cigars, just enough to get him through the rest of the day.

"Beautiful day," the tobacconist said.

"Oh? Yes." The chief inspector snipped the end of one of the cigars. "If a large man with a suitcase comes in, you let the police know."

The tobacconist's brow crumpled into a question, leaving the smile alone on his mouth.

The chief inspector turned to leave the store without answering the unspoken question.

Outside, Pelleter scanned the square almost without thinking, the old habit of a longtime policeman. But nothing registered out of the ordinary. He lit his cigar, and his muscles relaxed with the first inhalation of smoke. He rolled his neck, feeling the now reassuring pain in his shoulders. He wondered if Fournier had heard yet of the warden's arrest. What about Mahossier, who seemed to know everything?

The chief inspector's nostrils flared, and he bit down on his cigar. Yes, perhaps it wasn't quite finished. Maybe Letreau was near satisfied, but what had Mahossier said, that Pelleter was to find who had taken the bodies out of the prison and the madman would supply the names of who had made them bodies in the first place?

Pelleter shook away the thought of having anything

more to do with the man. He headed back across the square, forced to nod to the old men at the war monument again as though he had not just seen them minutes before.

Over the course of the afternoon, Pelleter regretted having bought cheap cigars. He regretted having bought only three cigars.

The reports came in from the search party, from the roadblocks, from Lambert at the train station.

Nothing.

# 15.

## *Dinner with Friends*

"Come then, shall we?" Chief Letreau called across the station, emerging from his office, already arranging his overcoat on his shoulders.

Pelleter looked up without seeing his friend. His gaze shifted to the floor; he shook his head and pulled himself to his feet.

The long uneventful afternoon had unsettled the chief inspector, eradicating any sense of progress from the morning. Pelleter now felt certain that Passemier was within his grasp if only he could remember the correct detail, but he had been through his notebook no less than ten times without stumbling upon the answer.

Letreau gave orders to be followed in his absence. "The warden's wife will be bringing Soldaux and the warden dinner. She can stay with them while they eat. But then she must go. Don't let her give you any trouble."

Letreau clapped his hands on Pelleter's shoulders and kneaded them like a coach with a prizefighter. Pelleter shrugged away, wincing from the pain of his injury.

But the chief of police didn't see, already at the door, turning to check whether Pelleter was following him.

Pelleter said to the desk officer, "When my man calls, tell him to hold his position. I'll be there soon."

Outside the sun had already fallen out of sight but the

sky had not yet started to darken. There was an easiness about Letreau as he guided them towards his home. It was the relaxed confidence of a man of authority in control of his domain, something that had been missing in the chief of police since their initial trip to the baker's days before. For Pelleter, on his walk home after work, he always felt the crush of responsibility, the city and its inhabitants too large to fathom, his job to keep out the barbarians by building a gate out of toothpicks. But here, the normal order of business was petty theft and vandalism, and Letreau currently had most of the regular perpetrators conducting a search for a suspect on his behalf.

A girl—or was she a young woman—collided with Letreau in the doorway of his house.

"Whoa there," Letreau said, wrapping his arms around her. "Where do you think you're going?"

The girl ducked her head, crossed her wrists over her chest, and leaned shoulder-first into Letreau, allowing herself to be embraced. "I've just come to borrow some salt, Uncle."

Letreau waddled in place, rotating them in the doorway so that his back was to the open house and the girl was on the street side. He looked at Pelleter over the girl's head, his eyes gleaming, and asked her, "You don't want to stay for dinner? We've got an important guest from the city."

The girl realized that she was being watched by a stranger, and she pulled herself away, straightening her frock with one hand, a teacup held in the other. She slid her hair behind first one ear and then the other with an unconscious turn of her fingers. "We've already started cooking at home," the young woman said, for Pelleter saw that she was a young woman. "But thank you, Uncle."

Letreau pressed his smile between closed lips, and nodded once. "Yes, of course."

The young woman smiled at Pelleter, then her uncle, and darted off, grabbing at her skirt with her free hand.

"My wife's sister's daughter," Letreau said, stepping into his house.

Pelleter watched the young woman hurry along the street for a moment. She went to a house several doors down and pushed her way inside. The sight of her made him think of Clotilde Rosenkrantz, and then in turn of Passemier. Why was he so preoccupied? Why couldn't he feel some of the closure that Letreau clearly felt? If the man was to be found, he would be found.

The chief inspector followed Letreau into the house. The smell of cooking filled the space, chicken and rosemary.

Letreau had gone back to the kitchen, and Pelleter followed.

"Oh, good you're home," his wife said, lifting a roasting pan out of a coal stove with two leather potholders. "Everything is ready. You can sit down."

A gnarled old woman with no teeth blinked and smiled at Pelleter, tasting her lips.

"My mother-in-law," Letreau said by way of an introduction. "She's deaf."

"Would you get her seated?" Madame Letreau said. "She insists on helping, but she's always just in the way. Alice was just here."

"I saw her on the way out."

The name came back to him, and Pelleter realized that he had met the girl on one of his previous visits, only she had been a child then, and Letreau had doted on her. Nothing else had appeared to change.

"Inspector Pelleter, you've decided to have a real meal finally."

"Madame Letreau. Through no fault of your husband, I assure you."

The table was a small round butcher block in an ill-lit corner of the kitchen. There were four wicker chairs, the wicker in two of them broken through in places—Madame Letreau made sure to arrange them so that she and her husband took those chairs. There was just space for the four of them to have the roast chicken, boiled beets and potatoes that reminded Pelleter once again of how many days this business had kept him from home.

"So you've arrested the warden and one of the guards," Madame Letreau said, still on her feet, making sure her mother was settled with her precut meal.

Letreau looked put out that his wife had already heard his news, but he regathered himself, chewing heartily a purplish mass of beets and potatoes. "Yes. It seems thanks to Inspector Pelleter that things aren't a complete mess."

Madame Letreau's mother stared across the table at the chief inspector with a blank smile.

"That's certainly good news," Madame Letreau said without looking up, and then, "Eat!", gesturing to her mother, who frowned, shifted back and forth on her seat, and shrugged her shoulders. "Eat!" Madame Letreau took her own seat, and in a moment, the old woman leaned forward to take her fork in her hand.

"We still have no idea who murdered all of those men," Inspector Pelleter said, troubled by Letreau's good spirits.

"Unimportant," Letreau said, sticking a hunk of chicken in his mouth. "The only crime committed as far as I'm concerned was improper disposal of human remains, and we have people in custody for that and will soon have the last man as well. And with a cold murder solved as a bonus. If Fournier or whoever's in charge out at the prison now feels they have murders to solve, those are on their hands."

Pelleter saw how it was going to be. He heard Madame Rosenkrantz saying it didn't matter if they ever found out who had killed her father. That it wouldn't change anything.

"Didn't Mahossier tell you that he knew who had killed the prisoners?" Madame Letreau said.

"It's never clear what Mahossier has told you," Pelleter said, curt.

"I must not understand," Madame Letreau said.

The four of them fell to eating. Much of the old woman's meal fell back on her plate. Letreau's good mood had been tempered, and Pelleter's troubled mood had grown.

"You're going to return home tonight?" Madame Letreau said after the silence became awkward.

"Or tomorrow."

"Oh?" Letreau said, setting his hand down on the table and looking at Pelleter in surprise.

Pelleter didn't elaborate, but took another bite of the

chicken. The food was excellent and he told Madame Letreau.

"Who is he?" Madame Letreau's mother leaned over and asked her daughter in a loud voice.

"A policeman from the city," Madame Letreau shouted.

Letreau smiled, but it was clear he was uncomfortable and embarrassed by his mother-in-law. "So you may stay until tomorrow. I'm glad to have you. I can't thank you enough for this."

Pelleter drank his wine. "There's something I'm missing."

"I always feel like that," Letreau said.

Pelleter tried to hide a scowl with another bite of food.

They were quiet again. The old woman was still fixed on the chief inspector, who suddenly remembered the bruise on his face. His hand went up to it self-consciously.

The old woman nodded, and her smile deepened, her lips falling further into her mouth.

"Do you think we'll find this man?" Letreau asked, as he had before at the station, but it was only to say something, to fill the silence.

"He'll be found. It's only a question of when."

"I don't really believe he's in town anymore," Letreau said.

"Is he dangerous?" Madame Letreau said.

"Well…" Letreau started, and then looked at Pelleter, seeing his face.

"Yes," the chief inspector said. He was ready to go, but dinner was not yet over. They were each only halfway through their meal, each on their first glass of wine. But this was beginning to feel like a poor use of time. Letreau thought Passemier was gone. He was probably right, but somehow Pelleter was not entirely convinced.

There were noises out on the street, distant shouts, and the sound of a dog barking.

The two policemen shifted in their seats, and the silence at the table changed in tone, from awkwardness to expectancy. The old woman was unaware of the sounds coming from the street, and she sat with the same complacent smile.

Letreau pushed back from the table as the shouting grew louder. "Damn it," he said, throwing his napkin onto the table.

The old woman looked up at him, still smiling. Madame Letreau continued to eat as though nothing was happening.

Pelleter knew that he was not leaving that night.

The sound grew louder. Letreau had opened the front door. His voice joined the shouting.

Pelleter stood up, and left the kitchen without saying anything to either of the women.

There was a young police officer standing outside the front door talking with Letreau. Behind him were several of the rough-looking youths who had answered the call for the search party earlier that afternoon.

A dog was barking, but wasn't visible. The dusk was heavy.

"I'm sorry, sir," the young officer said.

"No, it's absolutely right."

"It's really not necessary."

"No, no, I insist," Letreau said, stepping back. He saw Pelleter there. "They're searching this block now, house by house, and they want to search mine as per my orders to skip nobody. It's only right."

The officer stood in the doorway looking at the two senior officers, unsure of how to proceed.

"Come on," Letreau said.

The officer stepped in, and two of the young men with rifles hurried in from the street behind him. They fanned out in what had clearly become a practiced maneuver over the course of the day, one man heading directly for the stairs, another heading for the kitchen and the back of the house, while the police officer stood at the front door.

The officer wiped his hands along his pants legs. "I'm really sorry, sir."

"No, it's quite right." But now that the men were in his house, his jaw was set, his teeth clenched, his shoulders tensed. "I haven't been upstairs myself yet. What better place to hide than here."

There was laughing in the street. Banging on a door. The dog was still barking. Someone yelled, "Shut up."

The sound of the man upstairs could be heard through the ceiling. Doors banged.

"Sorry, *mesdames*," the man in the kitchen could be heard to say.

Letreau was stick-straight.

Pelleter felt the invasion too. Their awkward dinner had been their space, and now these strangers had come in and taken it away from them. He saw the house as a police officer now, not as a guest. The living room was

small with three men standing in it. The arms of the
chairs and loveseat were worn thin, showing the wood
beneath the fabric. The framed photographs on the walls
were askew, both in relation to each other and to the
floor. A water stain browned and bulged the paint in one
corner.

The man came from the back of the house. There was
still banging upstairs.

"You've had no luck?" Letreau said, although this was
apparent.

"No, sir."

"Okay, then."

The man came down from upstairs, taking the stairs so
fast as to be almost falling down them.

"Nice place you got, Chief," the man said, cigarette
bobbing between his lips.

Letreau said nothing as the man passed by him and
outside. Something was said, and there was a fresh burst
of laughter as though the group were out drinking instead
of searching for a fugitive.

The officer, embarrassed at the lack of control he had
over his men, many of whom were his age or older, tried
to smile and said, "Good night, sir," and then turned and
left.

The group moved off down the block in the direction
of Alice's house. Letreau stood by the open door, his body
still rigid, probably also thinking that his niece would soon
be visited by the same invasion, but he held his ground,
no doubt reminding himself of equity, and how he would
rather this intrusion than the fugitive on the run.

Letreau closed the door, and when he spoke his voice

was pinched. "They're certainly being thorough," he said. He started for the kitchen, stopped at the bottom of the steps as though he were considering going upstairs to check for any damage or missing belongings, but instead he continued on to the kitchen where his wife and mother-in-law were still eating the dinner they had prepared.

At the table, Letreau sat upright, staring straight ahead, attacking his food. His breathing was shallow. Any jocularity from before was gone. The two women did not react. When Madame Letreau was finished eating, she stood with her plate and her mother's and began to clean up. Pelleter wondered how typical a dinner this was for the household, as he chewed his food on the side of his face opposite the bruise.

It was a chill April night that made any hope for spring seem rash and ill founded. The cold was made more oppressive by the memory of the beautiful day.

Pelleter found Lambert beside the railroad tracks with his arms crossed, his hands shoved into his armpits, the collar of his overcoat bunched up around the bottom of his hairline. Another officer, whom Pelleter recognized as Arnaud, stood unfazed by the weather beside the city policeman.

The chief inspector knew that his friend was exaggerating his discomfort for effect.

"You misplaced your bag, I see," Lambert said.

"I'm not going home tonight."

"Why does that not surprise me?"

"I've got to go out to the prison one more time to see

Mahossier. Mahossier..." Pelleter trailed off and looked at Arnaud, who was gazing down the tracks, vague white lines of reflected moonlight. He was either not paying attention to the chief inspector's conversation or trying to show that he wasn't. "The official investigation is over here. They're going to finish their search for Passemier, put his name and description out on the wire, and ignore the murders. The warden was right about one thing. Nobody cares about a bunch of prisoners getting killed."

"So why do you have to see Mahossier?"

"Something he said...And he started this whole thing." Pelleter looked down the track for the train. "I hate that man."

Lambert let out a long breath. "God, it's cold."

"It's not too bad," Arnaud said.

"Are you going to be all right out here for the night?" Pelleter said.

"A night standing out in the country in the cold was exactly what I was hoping for," Lambert said.

"How have you been working it?"

"When the train's coming, Arnaud goes to the other side of the track, we watch the length of the train, walk along it, and then watch it until the train pulls out. Not that we're going to be able to see anything in the dark."

"I'll help."

"You don't expect there's anything to be seen?"

"No."

"He's already gone?"

Pelleter took a moment before he answered. "No, I don't think he's gone yet."

Lambert knew the chief inspector well enough to remain silent after that comment, to allow his boss to think.
The three men stood in the cold, not as though they were
waiting for something, but as though standing itself was
their purpose, and they could stand forever.

At last the rails bean to sing, the high-pitched hum of
the approaching train, and the pinprick star beyond
where the tracks were visible appeared. Arnaud moved
up the slight rise to the tracks, crossed over the metal
rails, and then fell away up to mid-thigh on the other side.

The train sounded its whistle.

The light grew brighter, and more of the engine began
to take form in the moonlight, the black plume of smoke
rising from the smokestack blotting out the night sky
above. The train wheels could be heard themselves now,
clacking.

Pelleter pointed, and Lambert went ahead without any
other command, jogging down the track so that he would
be where the train would stop, near the freight cars.

Pelleter looked around at the darkness surrounding
the nearest brush and buildings, but nothing moved.

The train slowed, the clack of the wheels changing
rhythm to a labored chug.

Pelleter realized that he had awaited the train with the
warden on it only that morning, and he had to consciously
remind himself that he had not yet been in Verargent
a week.

The train came to a stop.

Pelleter stepped right up alongside the engine, the
sooty smoke making the air hot. Lambert jogged the
length of the train towards him, and Pelleter watched

behind his officer to see if anything moved in the shadows.

Several men got off of the train, talking loudly to one another.

Lambert was shaking his head before he even reached Pelleter.

Pelleter saw nothing either. He looked at the men arriving, and recognized two of them as reporters from the city. So they had finally decided that the incidents at Verargent were something they should get some first-hand information on. He was surprised it had taken them this long, but perhaps the arrest of the warden of a national prison was the first real news. He was glad that they were not yet on the job, that they were idly joking with one another rather than looking around, and so he avoided having to refuse any interviews right now. It would not be as easy tomorrow.

"Nothing, Chief," Lambert said. "This guy's gone. You sure we need to stick around until tomorrow?"

Pelleter nodded.

Arnaud appeared from around the other side of the train.

"Anything?" Pelleter said.

"Nothing, sir."

The train conductor was looking out the window down at the policemen. Pelleter waved him on. His head disappeared, and the train started up its slow steady chuffing, shuddering once, and then pulling slowly away from the station.

"We're done here for the night," Pelleter said. "Go get some rest, and be sure to be back for the morning train."

The three men turned in the direction of town. The reporters were already gone.

The policemen walked in silence. The sound of the retreating train ushered them to their respective beds, a quiet shush after awhile and then gone.

Pelleter promised himself he'd be on that train to-morrow.

The chief inspector lay in bed for a moment after waking but before getting up. This was uncharacteristic of him, who usually was half-dressed before he realized that he was awake. He had had quite a lot of difficulty falling asleep the night before, waiting for the phone to ring with news of the search, certain that it wouldn't, and still plagued with the idea that there was something he was missing, that Passemier was in town and he should know exactly where. Now the sun bled through the curtains, lighting the too-familiar room, and the prospect of another trip to Malniveau Prison made Pelleter feel old.

He ran through it in his head again. Friday night Passe-mier followed him to the Rosenkrantz house but left off once Pelleter spotted him. Saturday the chief inspector had his lineup at the prison where Passemier tried to act tough and impressive. That same night Passemier followed the detective and attacked him when he thought he was cornered. Sunday Passemier packed his suitcase and went on the run.

The facts told him nothing.

Downstairs, the Verargent Hotel's lobby had become a journalists' salon. The four men from the train last night had been joined by three others who must have come by car, and right in the center of the group talking louder than all the others was Philippe Servières.

"Inspector Pelleter!" It was one of the city boys. "You feel like answering some questions?"

The group had fallen silent and turned expectantly to the chief inspector, retrieving notebooks and pencils from coat pockets.

"It sure took you all long enough to get down here," the chief inspector said, without breaking his stride.

"What do you expect with this Richard-Lenoir business?"

Pelleter stopped, and turned to the man who had spoken. "What are you talking about?

"You haven't heard?"

"You really have been out in the middle of nowhere," one of the reporters from the train said.

"Countess Richard-Lenoir murdered her three children, the count, and then shot herself on their yacht down in Nice. You can't hardly expect a few rotting corpses to compete with that."

"I was keeping all the papers informed of the situation here," Servières said.

Some of the reporters seemed to smirk at that.

"Now with the warden in it…"

Pelleter looked at the group of them with disgust, and then turned to go.

"Inspector Pelleter…"

"What does Mahossier have to do with this?"

"Did the warden commit the murders?"

Pelleter turned around, and the group of reporters that had surged towards the door after him tripped over each other as they came to a stop. "If you want a story, go out and find the missing prison guard," Pelleter said, and with that he left the hotel.

The weather was clear, but with some of the night's chill still in the air. Verargent Square was busy with Monday morning activity, the doors to the shops open to the good weather, women out with their shopping baskets on their arms. A few of the men from the search party were smoking near the war monument, their rifles leaning against the base of the statue. Their eyes stared straight ahead. Gone was the joking and laughing of the day before.

Pelleter cut through the traffic to the tobacconist's, knowing he would not make it through the day without a supply of cigars.

The tobacconist said nothing about the previous night's search. He sold Pelleter his cigars in silence—still machine-rolled, but a better brand—and Pelleter lit one before leaving the shop.

In the square by the monument the small group of ragged men with guns had grown. Some of the other pedestrians glanced at them as they went by. Had Letreau called for a resumption of the search this morning?

Pelleter returned to the thought that the Perreaux children had been lost in a field. If they hadn't found Passemier yet and didn't know where he was going to be, there were too many places for him to hide. They wouldn't find him.

Pelleter smoked and watched the square, not yet ready to join the day.

He saw Rosenkrantz in the little café, standing at the

counter with a coffee cup in his hand. The chief inspector was surprised that the American would be away from his wife after spending so many days concerned for her safety. He thought again how hard it was to know people as he watched the American gesture with his cup, the broad open movement of a satisfied man.

Letreau was crossing from the police station to where the small group of men was still growing.

Several more men walked towards the group, although it appeared as though it was out of curiosity rather than any interest in joining in the search. Pelleter recognized the nervous form of Benoît, the baker, who still wore his white apron, his hair grayed by flour. He must be coming to hear if there was any news.

The chief inspector's nose flared. Passemier had followed him and he had let him get away! Such overconfidence!

He shook his head, blowing out smoke, and watched Letreau give new orders.

But why had the man followed him, Pelleter asked himself yet again. To what end? Not only would there have been no reason for Passemier to follow him, in fact it would only have been a risk.

Pelleter's head snapped back to Rosenkrantz. There was a man standing in the café doorway now, one of the reporters, and the few people inside were turned to listen to him, soon ready to give any information he would want to hear.

Pelleter began to walk.

When the chief inspector had arrived at the Rosenkrantz home the night Rosenkrantz was drunk, he had come by taxi. If Passemier had been on foot, how could he have followed him?

Pelleter began to hurry.

He had assumed at the time that he'd been followed. But the prison guard must have already been waiting at the Rosenkrantz home.

The reporter was inside the café now, standing at the counter beside Rosenkrantz.

And at the hospital—

Madame Rosenkrantz had been with him when he spotted Passemier following, before the guard fled and then attacked.

Rosenkrantz was yelling at the reporter now, his gesticulations clear even from a distance and through the window.

If Passemier had been at the Rosenkrantz home one night and then at the hospital where Madame Rosenkrantz had been for the past several days the next...

Pelleter was running now, past the café, in the direction of the American writer's house.

The warden and his two cohorts had gambled that the dead prisoners' families wouldn't make inquiries. But when Passemier found out that Meranger's daughter lived right here in town, he must have wanted to make sure that no questions would be asked. Which meant Clotilde...

Someone in the square noticed him, and there were shouts behind him, but the chief inspector didn't look back.

No, Pelleter told himself, even as he ran. He had to be wrong. But it made too much sense. He had thought that for the last few days the prison guard had been following him. But what if the fugitive had been after Clotilde, and the chief inspector had just happened to be there?

Pelleter's cigar had gone out, clenched as it was, forgotten, in his hand.

No, he had not just been overconfident. He had been blind. Now he hoped he wasn't too late. Because now Clotilde was home. And she had a car, which Passemier badly needed, and she was on the edge of town.

And as her husband was here at the café, arguing with the reporter—

She was all alone.

# 16.

## *Clotilde-ma-Fleur*

Clotilde-ma-Fleur was troubled by the sun. It had come up that morning already bright and clean. It was the kind of spring day in which everything existed in equal calm, the sun intense but not hot, the air cool but still. The house was suffused with light.

It was hard in the face of such perfection to not feel uplifted. Her husband had fallen to his knees before her when she came into the house two nights ago. He wrapped his arms around her waist and pressed his face against her stomach. It was only by a single intake of breath that she knew he was crying. He had then stood, picking her up in the same movement and carried her up the stairs to their bedroom. She had been afraid that he would hurt himself.

The next morning, he grinned at her in the sunlit dining room throughout breakfast, and doted on her all through the day. The attention made it difficult for her to look at him. This morning, after enduring a full day of such attentions, she sent him out under the pretext that she needed to do a proper housecleaning after her negligence of the past few days, but in fact she wanted a chance to check herself.

She did clean. The kitchen first, washing the dishes from breakfast, and then the counter, the sink, the floor, working up a fine sweat and a warm feeling in her chest. Her mind was clear with the task, but then it would come—my father is dead—and she would stop. Her sorrow was a wave of exhaustion. In the pauses between the peaks, she could raise herself before being knocked down again.

She was upstairs in their room now, changing the linens on the bed, humming in her task, no particular tune, just a wispy tone as she exhaled. She tightened the corner of the sheet at the head of the bed, pulling the excess material up in a right triangle before tucking it under the mattress and running her hand across the sheet to flatten it.

There was a noise downstairs, perhaps the door. She thought of calling to say that she was upstairs, but she was not quite ready to give up her solitude. She felt guilty about her inner calm, and felt unsure about herself if it were to break.

She walked around the bed, to tighten the sheet on the other side.

There was a loud crash downstairs as of a drawer being roughly closed and something tottering from a height. She stopped and stood up, looking at the stairs.

"Shem!" she called.

There was no reply.

She went to the window cut into the slanted ceiling, and looked out at the street. Their car was in the driveway—Shem hadn't taken it—but no one else was there, no car parked at the curb.

She thought she heard another drawer being closed.

She went to the top of the stairs, reaching her hand

out for the banister. She took a tentative step down. "Shem!"

There was a movement, someone walking. Why didn't he answer?

She went down. When her head fell below the height of the upper floor, she stopped, her free hand going to her chest.

There was a strange suitcase standing just inside the door, which was ajar.

She tried to remember if she had left the door open, listening so carefully that she could hear her own breathing. She hadn't. And that suitcase. The light from the door cast a severe shadow from the suitcase on the floor. She stepped down again.

"Shem, where are you!"

It was nothing, she told herself, an unexpected friend, even as she remembered that policeman's face from two nights before. She started to hurry down the stairs, watching her feet so she didn't trip.

"Lover!"

She stepped onto the first floor, and turned herself around the banister to head back towards her husband's study. There were quick steps behind her then, and she began to turn, "You scared—"

Strong arms went around her shoulders, and a blade flashed in her peripheral vision. Her throat closed and her head went light.

"Hello, Madame Rosenkrantz." The breath of the voice was hot on her ear. "Now, where do you keep the keys to your car?"

⚹

The car was still in the drive. That was the first thing
Pelleter noticed. He wished he could have Lambert with
him, or even Martin, but he was afraid there wasn't time.

He stopped just short of the property, at the edge of
the fence, breathing hard but still in control. The front
door was open, but he couldn't see anything inside. There
were no sounds either. The natural thing would be to go
right up to the front door as though he were just there for
a visit and to see how it played out. But he didn't like the
idea of giving the man any advantage if he was here, and
now Pelleter was certain he was. How had he thought
that Passemier would go for the circuitous route, bypassing
the roadblocks by going through the fields? He should
have known that a man like Passemier—a man who would
attack a police officer—would opt for a hostage and try to
force his way through. Now the most important thing was
to get Madame Rosenkrantz out unhurt.

The chief inspector sped along the side of the fence,
retrieving his revolver and holding it ahead of him. He
couldn't make anything out in the windows as he passed.
He let himself through the back gate.

There was no one in the backyard.

The search party had seen the chief inspector running, so there should be men on the way. The trick was to
assess the situation if possible, and to prevent Passemier
from getting away if necessary.

He hurried to the back door, standing off to the side
with his back to the wall of the house. There was a small
semi-circular window made of three panes in the upper

portion of the back door. The chief inspector allowed himself a quick look.

The hall was shadowed, all of the light coming from the open door at the other end. All the chief inspector could be certain of was that it was empty.

Pelleter reached across the door and tried the handle. It was unlocked. The hinges were mercifully silent.

He entered the house with his gun ahead of him. It took a moment for his eyes to adjust to the lower light. It was bright in the house, but not quite as bright as outside.

There was a suitcase at the end of the hall near the open door. Passemier's, surely. Where would the Rosenkrantzes be going? Monsieur Rosenkrantz had seemed in no hurry back in the square. The chief inspector listened for sounds, but the only sounds were the normal noises of an old country home talking to itself as it aged.

The door to the study on his right was closed. He reached down across his body with his left hand, still holding the revolver pointed towards the front door, and turned the doorknob. The study was as he had seen it two days before, messy and empty.

He left the door open, turned, and brought his head close to the kitchen door, listening.

There was nothing.

He pushed his way into the kitchen. It smelled of strong soap, which stung his nostrils and made his eyes water. This room was empty as well.

He stopped beside the center counter.

Had there been steps upstairs?

He looked up. The creak of a board.

He crossed the kitchen in two silent steps, but before he could push open the swinging door that led into the dining room, he heard the erratic drumming of feet stumbling down the steps. There was a soft cry and a man's voice.

Pelleter brought up his gun and gripped it with both hands.

Somebody yelled, "Clotilde!"

The front door slammed.

Pelleter rushed into the dining room, his gun extended, and hurried past the table towards the front door, but stopped before he got there. The scene was framed in the dining room window as though it were a photograph.

Passemier had his back to the house with Clotilde part of the way in front of him, the suitcase now in his free hand, and the other one wrapped around her neck. Rosenkrantz was there, saying something and inching forward, almost at the front door of the automobile. From the slowness of the action, Pelleter knew that Passemier must have some kind of weapon in his hand.

Passemier began to move away from the house and toward the car, shoving Clotilde before him.

If the chief inspector came through the front door, Passemier would hear him at once, and then they would just be in a standoff, and either Clotilde was more likely to get hurt or they would be forced to let Passemier get away.

Pelleter ducked back into the kitchen and ran out the back door. His only chance was to come up behind Passemier unseen. He hurried around the other side of the house, which led down the drive, bringing the others

into view. As he did, the car horn sounded. Once. Twice.
Three times. Good man, Rosenkrantz.

Pelleter moved deliberately now, not wanting his footsteps to give him away even with the car horn blaring.

Passemier was yelling, "You cut that out. Cut that out
right now or I'll kill her!"

Pelleter was close enough that he could see the strain
in the muscles in the back of Passemier's neck. He could
also see the knife clasped in Passemier's closed fist.

Rosenkrantz stopped pressing the horn, holding up
his hands, saying, "Okay," in that American accent of his.

"I'll kill her," Passemier said again.

Pelleter kicked at the back of Passemier's knee while
grabbing at his knife hand, causing the man to lose his
balance, and allowing Clotilde to duck away.

Passemier immediately began to pull his knife hand,
and the chief inspector felt himself dragged forward, but
instead of resisting, he allowed himself to be pulled,
raising his knee so that it landed in Passemier's stomach,
doubling the man over and causing him to loosen his grip
on the knife.

The chief inspector chopped at the prison guard's wrist
with the butt of his gun, and the knife clattered to the
ground, but Passemier, still doubled over, swung both
hands over his head, throwing Pelleter's balance off just
enough that the chief inspector had to fall back on the
hood of the car with one elbow to keep from tumbling to
the ground.

Passemier was around the edge of the car in an instant.

Inspector Pelleter came up with his gun raised, but
the Rosenkrantzes were between him and the fugitive.

Rosenkrantz pulled Clotilde out of the way. Pelleter ran around them.

Passemier had turned left, away from town. By the time Pelleter reached the street, the prison guard had realized his mistake, zigzagging down the center of the street as the buildings grew further apart from one another, providing no place to hide.

Pelleter called, "Stop!"

The big man was staggering, still winded from the blow to his stomach, his bulk awkward in the first place. He didn't look back. He must have seen the roadblock one hundred yards ahead, where the last of the town's outlying buildings gave way to pure farmland. Pelleter didn't want him to cut into the fields. The inspector raised his revolver, and shot into the air.

Passemier looked back at the noise, tripping, but regaining his balance before going down.

The men at the roadblock had heard the shot and recognized it for what it was, and they had begun to run towards them.

Passemier saw that he was about to be surrounded, and he chose to turn around and charge Pelleter.

Pelleter paused, and took aim with his revolver. But the men from the roadblock were too close now. He couldn't risk hitting one of Letreau's men. He reholstered his gun, and bent his knees as the large man came.

The young men from the roadblock were almost on him now, too. They had begun to yell, "Stop! Police! Stop!"

Passemier dropped a shoulder.

Pelleter watched the other man's eyes, but they were pinioned straight ahead.

"Stop! Police!"

Passemier was on him. Pelleter tried to step aside and trip the guard, but Passemier anticipated the move, traveling with Pelleter, barreling full-tilt into the chief inspector's chest, knocking the wind out of Pelleter, whose vision went white. He barely managed to keep his feet.

Passemier pushed past the chief inspector, and on towards town.

The younger officers were there now, passing Pelleter.

Pelleter pulled out his revolver again, still gasping for breath. The air felt cold and dry along the back of his throat. "Move!"

He shot in the air.

The young men looked back, and Pelleter had already taken aim. One of the officers called to his companions, dropping to the ground.

Pelleter shot.

Passemier stumbled. Then began to run again. But now it was more of a loping hop.

One of the younger officers jumped to his feet, and was on Passemier in no time. He yelled at Passemier, but Passemier just turned and swiped at him.

Pelleter was there. He saw that his shot had been good. There was blood on Passemier's pantleg at his left calf. Pelleter kicked for the spot, and Passemier went down.

Pelleter was on top of the large man, a knee in the prison guard's back, and his revolver to Passemier's head.

"Your friends are waiting for you," Pelleter said.

He used his free hand to retrieve his handcuffs, roughly pulling Passemier's hands back, first left, then right.

Passemier had too often been on the other side of the equation to struggle at that point. He knew it would go badly for him, and so he let his body go limp.

Pelleter looked up. The young police officer had been Martin. "Good job."

Martin tried to keep a straight face, but he couldn't hold back his smile. "Thank you, sir."

Further along the street, in front of their house, the Rosenkrantzes were holding each other, Monsieur Rosenkrantz watching Pelleter, Passemier, and the police over Clotilde's head. His expression was of a man defeated instead of triumphant. Verargent was supposed to be their safe haven. It had not been that.

Letreau was beaming. "Well, we wrapped this whole thing up thanks to you! You really saved me."

Pelleter laughed. "You'll just have to return the favor next time you visit me."

Lambert rolled his eyes at Pelleter, and the chief inspector gave his man a stern expression.

The chief of police opened the top drawer of his desk and came out with three cigars. He handed them across the desk to the two other men. Pelleter's heart leapt at the sight of it. He had a headache he needed to smoke so badly.

"Now if someone found out who killed all of those prisoners…" Letreau said, but he was still smiling. "But that, my friends is a prison problem. Illegally disposing of remains—that one we solved. And an old murder on top of that."

Pelleter filled his lungs with the tobacco smoke. The cigar was not quite as good as the ones he was used to, the flavor a bit ashy, but it felt good anyway.

Letreau blew a series of broken smoke rings and then adjusted himself in his chair, looking down at his desk. "I really can't thank you enough."

Pelleter nodded.

"This whole business..." Letreau shook his head.

"I still should go out to the prison one last time, although I hate to do it," Pelleter said.

Letreau waved it away. "It's Fournier's problem. His problem."

Pelleter frowned, and tried to convince himself that was true. Really, how had any of this been his problem? "Don't be surprised if Fournier manages to solve at least some of those stabbings."

There was a knock at the open office door. All three men looked up.

An officer said, "Warden Fournier is on the phone, sir."

"Warden!" Letreau said. "He does move fast."

"Assistant Warden, sir, I'm sorry."

Letreau grabbed up the phone from his desk. "You heard our good news?" Letreau's brow furled. "What! When?"

Lambert looked at Pelleter who just shrugged, enjoying his cigar.

"We'll be out." Letreau hung up the phone. "There's been another stabbing. It's Mahossier."

# 17.

## *Mahossier in the Infirmary*

The infirmary had emptied now. It had been a flurry of activity for the last hour as the doctor and nurse saw to their new patient's wounds, and various law officials were in and out, overwhelmed by the continued excitement of the day. Pelleter had asked Fournier for his chance to speak with the prisoner before he left, and Fournier had agreed, standing guard with Lambert outside of the infirmary door.

The man who had been stabbed four days before was still in a bed across the room. His color had returned, and he was sitting up in the bed without a problem. He would be returned to his cell later that day. He would have been returned already if it had not been for this new stabbing.

Pelleter sat beside Mahossier's bed.

"How's Madame Pelleter?" Mahossier said.

His voice was weak, but Pelleter knew from the doctor that Mahossier's wounds were superficial. His weakness was a calculated act, like so much with Mahossier.

Pelleter ignored the familiar question.

"I hear that our warden is no longer our warden."

"Are you happy about that?"

Mahossier shrugged. "We can't plan what life gives us. We have to take it as it comes."

Pelleter narrowed his eyes, trying to discover the best way to approach his topic. With Mahossier, it was never an easy matter of discovering the truth unless Mahossier decided to give it to you. "Fournier will no doubt be warden now."

"A pity." Mahossier seemed uninterested in that.

"That one's going to live," Pelleter said, indicating the man across the room.

"Oh, he's going to die, inspector. We're all going to die. We're dying right now, as we speak."

Pelleter's face grew dark. He had uncovered too much already. He didn't have the energy or the patience to philosophize with a multiple murderer. "You killed those men."

"What men?" Mahossier said, his eyebrows raised in surprise.

"Those prisoners."

Mahossier's face changed to a sly smile. "Not my type."

"Or you had them killed. You wanted to get at Fournier, and you figured that a lot of dead bodies soon after he showed up was going to make things difficult for him. You didn't expect that the murders would be covered up by other people for other reasons, and so when nothing happened, you had me brought in to stir things up."

"You do like telling stories," Mahossier said. "I hear you've been telling them a lot the last few days."

Pelleter didn't rise to the bait, or ask how Mahossier always was so well informed. He went on.

"You're the one who called 'here' when Meranger was already dead. Your cell was next to his. You just wanted to throw further confusion into the mix."

Mahossier winced, as though suddenly struck with pain, but the gleam in his eyes made it clear that it was just an act.

"You've missed your mark. You've deposed the warden, and put the man you hated in charge."

Mahossier shrugged. "It is what it is."

Pelleter reached out, ready to push on the cuts across Mahossier's stomach. The prisoner didn't move, and Pelleter stopped short of actually hurting the man. "You cut yourself up to put suspicion somewhere else. But what happens when the killings stop now? Fournier won't let up, even if I'm gone."

"Who said the killings were going to stop?"

"Oh, I think they will. You've done enough."

"Perhaps."

Pelleter's eyes narrowed. Was that an admission? No, he could merely have meant that the killings would perhaps stop. Pelleter spoke through closed teeth. "Why?"

Mahossier smiled. "Why not?"

"Seven people!"

Pelleter could feel his face grow red with anger, and he forced himself to take a deep breath. It was wrong to let the man get to him. He was behind bars for life already. What more could be done to him?

Instead of responding to Pelleter's outrage, Mahossier said, "How *is* Madame Pelleter? It really is a shame you've never had any children."

Pelleter stood up at that. "Don't expect me to come next time you call for me." The inspector crossed the room for the door. Just as he reached it, Mahossier said behind him:

"We could all be dead by then, Inspector."

There was joy in the murderer's voice.

Pelleter went out into the hall, and walked past Lambert and Fournier without a word, heading for the front of the building. Seven people killed. And why? Because why not? And who actually held the knives might never be known.

Fournier overtook the chief inspector, and unlocked the doors in front of them as they walked, relocking them behind as they went.

Pelleter wondered if the American writer would use any of these events in his next book. It all seemed so unbelievable.

He reached for a cigar. They were at the front entrance to the prison.

"Thank you," Fournier called from behind him.

Pelleter didn't even wait to answer. He wanted to be out of Malniveau, free, away from locked doors.

THE
END

THE TWENTY-YEAR DEATH
Continues in

# *The*
# FALLING
# *Star*

Turn the page for
an exciting excerpt...

Merton Stein Productions was twelve square blocks enclosed by a ten-foot brick wall with pointed granite capstones every three yards. There was a lineup of cars at the main gate that backed out into the westbound passing lane of Cabarello Boulevard. Every five minutes or so the line advanced one car length. If you had urgent business you were no doubt instructed to take one of the other entrances. Since I had been directed to this one, I figured my business wasn't urgent.

It was just about noon on a clear day in the middle of July that wasn't too hot if you didn't mind the roof of your mouth feeling like an emery board. I smoked a cigarette and considered taking down the ragtop on my Packard to let in the mid-day sun. It was a question of whether it would be hotter with it closed or with it open. When it was my turn at the guard stand, I still hadn't decided.

A skinny young man in a blue security uniform stepped up to my open window without taking his eyes off of the clipboard in his hands. His face had the narrow lean look of a boy who hadn't yet grown into his manhood. His authority came from playing dress-up, but the costume wasn't fooling anyone, including himself. "Name," he said.

"Dennis Foster," I said. "You need to see proof?"

He looked at me for the first time. "You're not on the list."

"I'm here to see Al Knox."

He looked behind him, then out to the street, and finally settled back on his clipboard. "You're not on the list," he said again.

Before he could decide what to make of me, a voice said, "Get out of there." The kid was pushed aside and suddenly Al Knox was leaning on my door, wearing the same blue uniform, only many sizes larger. There was a metal star pinned to his chest and a patch below it that stated his name and the title Chief of Security. He stuck his hand in my face and I took it as he said, "Dennis. How the hell are you?"

"Covering the rent. How's the private security business?"

"Better than the public one. Give me a second, I'll ride in with you." He backed out of the window, told the skinny kid, "Open the gate, Jerry, this charmer's with me," and then crossed in front of my car in the awkward lope his weight forced on him. He opened the passenger door, grunted as he settled himself, and pulled the door shut. The sour smell of perspiration filled the car. He nodded his head and pointed at the windshield. "Just drive up Main Street here."

Jerry lifted the gate arm and I drove forward onto a two-way drive lined with two-story pink buildings that had open walkways on the second floors. There was a lot of activity on either side of the street, people in suits and people in painters' smocks and people in cavalry uniforms and women in tight, shiny skirts with lipstick that

matched their eyes. Three men in coveralls with perfectly
sculpted hair worked bucket-brigade-style unloading cos-
tumes from a truck. Workers walked in both directions
across a circular drive to the commissary. Knox directed me
to the third intersection, which had a street sign that said
Madison Avenue. Messrs. Young and Rubicam wouldn't
have recognized the place. We turned left, drove one
block over, past a building the size of an airplane hangar,
and made another left onto a boulevard with palm trees
in planters down the middle of the street. Here there was
a four-story building large enough to be a regional high
school. It had an oval drive and two flagpoles out front,
one flying Old Glory and the other flying a banner with
the Merton Stein crest on it. We drove past the oval and
pulled into a spot at the corner of the building beside a
row of black-and-white golf carts.

In front of us was a door with wired glass in the top
half that had the word "Security" painted on it in fancy
black-and-gold letters. I suppose the men who lettered
all those title cards in the old days needed something to
keep them busy now. To make doubly sure we knew where
we were, a sign on a metal arm above the door read
"Security Office." Knox started around the car to lead the
way when a woman's voice said something that wasn't
strictly ladylike. We looked, and three cars over a blonde
head bobbed into sight and then vanished again.

Knox pulled up his pants at the waistband as though
they might finally decide to go over his belly, and went
around to where we had seen the woman's head. I followed. Bent over, arms outstretched, the blonde made a
perfect question mark, an effect accentuated by the black

sundress she wore, which covered her from a spot just above her breasts to one just above her knees in a single fluid curve. She had on black high-heeled shoes with rhinestone decorative buckles, simple diamond stud earrings and a necklace with five diamonds set in gold across her white chest. In light of the earrings and the necklace, I allowed that the decorative buckles on the shoes might be real diamonds too. What she was bending over was the back seat of a new '41 Cadillac sedan. A pair of legs in wrinkled trousers was hanging out of the car, the man's heels touching the asphalt. She said the surprising word again, followed by "Tommy."

Knox said, "Do you need any help, Miss Merton?"

She straightened up. There was no sign of embarrassment on the sharp face that came into view, just annoyance and frustration. She brushed her hair back out of her face with one hand, and it stayed exactly where she wanted it, in an alluring sheet that just touched her shoulders. "Oh, Al. Can you help me get Tommy into the car again? He's passed out and he's too heavy for me."

Knox started forward and Miss Merton stepped back out of his way. She looked at me, and a smile formed on her face that suggested we shared a private secret. "Hello," she said. I didn't say anything. Her smile deepened. I didn't like that.

Knox wrestled Tommy's legs into the back seat, a process that involved some heavy breathing and maybe a few choice words under his breath too. At last he had the feet stowed in the well behind the driver's seat, and he slammed the door with satisfaction. "There you go, Miss Merton."

She turned to him, and said in a hard voice, "Tommy can't expect that I'll always go around cleaning up after him."

"No, ma'am," Knox said.

Miss Merton looked at me, gifted me with another smile, and then pulled open the door and poured herself into the driver's seat. Knox faced me, shaking his head but not saying anything as the Cadillac's engine caught and started. Only once the car was out of view did he say, under his breath, "Vera Merton. Daniel Merton's daughter. She's always around here getting into some trouble or other. The son doesn't usually even make it this far. He must have found himself caught out last night." He rolled his eyes and shook his head again. "The bosses, yeah?"

"The bosses," I said.

He gave a hearty laugh and slapped me on the back. "I'm telling you. This place is filled with crazies. Come on into my office, I'll fill you in."

The front room of the security office was a small, air conditioned, wood-paneled room with a metal office desk on which there were two telephones, a green-shaded lamp, a desk clock, a pen-and-ink set, a calendar blotter, and a message pad. There was a wooden rolling chair behind it, and three orange armchairs along the wall in front of it that had probably served time on one of the movie sets before their upholstery wore thin and they were re-assigned here. A middle-aged dark-haired man with a well-managed mustache looked up as we came in and then away as he saw it was Knox, who continued on through a door behind the desk marked "Private." This led to a narrow hallway off of which there were three more rooms. The first was an empty squad room with four desks, two couches, and a blackboard across one whole wall. The second was a kitchenette with a large table in the center and no less than three automatic coffee machines. Knox went into the third room, which was much like the first, only it had Knox's photographs on the wall. There were pictures taken with various movie stars, and pictures taken when he and I had been police, with Knox looking trim in his city uniform, and pictures taken when he was with the DA's office, looking less trim, but much thinner than he was now. "Close the door," he said, sitting down behind the desk.

I did and took the chair across from him.

"Sorry about the kid at the gate. We have a high turnover and it's either old retired cops like me or kids the academy turned away. The old guys can't take the heat in the box, so it goes to the kids. More than half of this job is managing my own staff."

I said I hadn't been bothered.

He nodded and puffed out his upper lip by forcing air into it. Then he moved his lips as though tasting something, and said, "This is a crap job I have for you, I just want to say that up front. It's a crap job, but the money's good and easy and I need someone I can trust."

"I'll just take my regular fee."

He shook his head. "No. I put in for fifty a day. And expenses, of course. This is the picture business, you take as much money as they'll give you."

"Let's leave that," I said. "What's the job?"

He puffed his lips again and rocked in his seat while

rubbing one hand back and forth on his blotter as though checking for splinters. He didn't want to tell. Telling me would make it real. At last he slapped his desk and said, "Oh, hell, you've already seen the kind of thing I have to deal with. These movie people live in a different world than guys like you and me."

"That's not what *Life* magazine says. Haven't you seen? Bogie built his own porch and Garbo sews all her clothes." Knox snorted at that. "Well, they love and hate and die like anyone else, don't they?"

"Sure, but they do it to the sound of violins, with their faces ten feet tall." He slapped his desk again. "If you have any sense of propriety left after being on the force, they sure knock it right out of you here. What do you know about Chloë Rose?"

"I've seen her pictures," I said.

"Well she manages that tortured beauty act from her pictures all the time in real life, too. And now we think maybe she's going crazy."

"What's she done?"

"Nothing much. Nothing besides the usual crying jags and mad demands and refusal to work that we get from any number of these women stars, including some who make the studio a lot less money than Chloë Rose. But now she thinks she's being followed. She's nervous all the time about it, and it's making it hard for Sturgeon to shoot the picture she's making. The studio has her on a five-year contract and there are three years to go, so there are people who are worried."

"Worried that she's actually being followed or worried that she thinks she's being followed?"

"Thinks." He drummed his fingers on the desk. "Maybe she is being followed, I don't know. But I tend to doubt it. These people are all paranoid. It's their sense of self-importance. Either way, I've managed to convince her well enough that I've got things under control here, that the only people on the lot are people who belong there. In truth, there's any number of ways to get onto the lot without us knowing. We have to throw people off the lot all the time, people who think they belong in pictures and are ready to prove it."

"So what do you want me to do?"

"Just follow her around when she's not on the set. Stakeout in front of her house at night."

"You want a bodyguard. I'm not a bodyguard."

"It's not a bodyguard job. I told you, she only thinks she's being followed. You just need to make her feel safe. For show."

"So I'm supposed to follow her around to make her feel better about somebody following her around?"

Knox held his hands wide and leaned back. "That's show business."

"Go back to Miss Rose's mystery man. It is a man, isn't it?"

"That's what she says."

"You said that you convinced her that the only people on the lot are people who belong on the lot. Why couldn't her tail be someone who belongs on the lot?"

"He could be. But don't point that out to her. She must not have thought of it."

"What's he supposed to look like?"

"Like every other man you've ever met, if you go by

her description. Medium height, dark hair, medium build. You'll talk to her about it. She'll fill you in."

"And she's seen him on the lot?"

"On the lot and off." He leaned forward. "That's if you believe her. I told you already. There's nobody following her. She's going dotty. There've been a batch of tantrums on the set. And her private life is worse than a paperback novel."

I raised an eyebrow.

He took a breath and let it out slowly. I waited.

"Her husband's Shem Rosenkrantz," he said. "He had a few books they liked in New York ten, fifteen years ago, but the last few years he's been hanging around here doing treatments that never get made. They never get made because he's too busy fooling around with the star- lets and he doesn't keep it a secret from his wife. This picture they're filming now is one he wrote and it's getting made because she's in it. And he's *still* having an affair with her co-star, this new girl called Mandy Ehrhardt. Meanwhile, Sturgeon, the director, has a thing for Rose, Missus Rosenkrantz if you're keeping score. Which might be fine if she wanted it too, but…"

"You sure he's not involved with this business?"

"Sturgeon? No. Sturgeon's on good behavior. And he's got reason to be. He had his last three productions fall apart in the middle of filming, and if he doesn't prove he can finish something, he's washed up here."

I mulled it over. "That all?"

"It's not enough?"

"Any old boyfriends that might be tailing her around?"

Knox said through his teeth, "Nobody's tailing her."

"Just for argument's sake."

Knox burst out laughing. "You haven't changed a bit. Still treat every job like it's a real case."

"What am I supposed to do when someone's paying me?"

"This is the picture business, boy. We all get paid for make-believe."

"Silly me," I said. "Always trying to do the right thing."

"You didn't learn anything when they threw you out of the department?"

"Sure, I learned that the law's something they print in books."

He held up his hands, palms out. "All right, all right. I'm not asking you to do anything that'll compromise your precious sense of ethics. All I want is for you to sit down with our star, get her to tell you her story, make lots of notes, and then tell her she doesn't need to worry. And then you can go get drunk in your car or sleep for all I care. It's just for a few days until the picture is done."

"I don't like it. I don't like that what you need's a body-guard, but what you went and got is me. I don't like a job that's not really a job, looking for a man that may or may not exist just to make some actress feel better. Send her to a doctor."

His face turned stormy. "I've already laid out our dirty laundry," he said, and opened his hands over his desk as though it were actually laid out there before us. "More than I ought to have said."

"You didn't tell me anything I couldn't have learned in a movie magazine."

"Come on, Foster. What's wrong with you? This is easy

money. I was scratching your back. You got so much work you can turn down fifty dollars a day? Since when?"

"I didn't say I wouldn't do it, I just said I didn't like it."

I could see the muscles of his face relax. He smiled and nodded. He had to be careful, Knox. The littlest thing would give him a coronary someday.

He stood up, his chair rolling backwards as it was freed from his weight. "I did tell you a few things they don't have in the glossies. And I'm sure you'll find out others. If I didn't know how discreet you are…"

And Knox did know. Back on the force, he would have lost his job more than once if it hadn't been for how discreet I was.

"Come on," he said, "let's go meet your client."

I stood too, but waited for Knox to come around the desk. "You're my client, Al."

He opened the door. "At least pretend that you're excited to meet a movie star."

# JOYLAND

## by **STEPHEN KING**

College student Devin Jones took the summer job at Joyland hoping to forget the girl who broke his heart. But he wound up facing something far more terrible: the legacy of a vicious murder, the fate of a dying child, and dark truths about life— and what comes after—that would change his world forever.

A riveting story about love and loss, about growing up and growing old—and about those who don't get to do either because death comes for them before their time—JOYLAND is Stephen King at the peak of his storytelling powers. With all the emotional impact of King masterpieces such as *The Green Mile* and *The Shawshank Redemption*, JOYLAND is at once a mystery, a horror story, and a bittersweet coming-of-age novel, one that will leave even the most hard-boiled reader profoundly moved.

### ACCLAIM FOR STEPHEN KING:

*"An immensely talented storyteller of seemingly inexhaustible gifts."*
— Interview

*"Stephen King is so widely acknowledged as America's master of paranormal terrors that you can forget his real genius is for the everyday."*
— New York Times

*"Stephen King is superb."*
— Time

**Available now at your favorite bookstore.
For more information, visit
www.HardCaseCrime.com**